Christmas
Treasure Box

Christmas Treasure Box

Shirley Burton

HIGH STREET PRESS

HIGH STREET PRESS
Niagara-on-the-Lake, ON, Canada
highstreetpress.com
shirleyburtonbooks.com
First printing 2018

Printed in the United States of America, Canada, UK, Australia, and global distribution in Europe, Asia, and South America.
Available in paperback, hardcover, and eBook formats.
Cover photo licensed Shutterstock.com.
Design and edit: Bruce Burton

Library and Archives Canada Cataloguing in Publication.

Burton, Shirley, 1950-, author
          Christmas treasure box/ Shirley Burton

Issued in print and electronic versions.
ISBN 978-1-927839-21-8 (pbk.). —ISBN 978-1-927839-22-5 (hardcover)
ISBN 978-1-927839-23-2 (ebook)

Home is the place where you feel the deepest affection, no matter where you are.

— Edmund Coke, 17th century proverb

WEAVER-WINSLOW-PERKINS
CONNECTIONS

Millicent Weaver m. (1939) Franklin Winslow
Ch. Madeleine Winslow (natural daughter of Jeremiah Hanson);
Ch. Adopted son, Stanley Winslow, adopted child

Jeremiah Hanson; bro. of Wilhelmina Hanson
Natural father of Millicent Winslow

Madeleine Winslow (b. 1939) m. Seymour Perkins
Ch. Pollyanna, Kate and Tim Perkins

Stanley Winslow m. Marjory Krane
Ch. Adopted son, Harris Winslow

Alexander Warner betrothed to Wilhelmina Hanson
Ch. Meredith Carver, mother of Jackson Tripp

1

December 1991

Snow had turned to sleet, and the visibility was almost fully diminished as Seymour and Maddie Perkins swerved on the icy highway. As visibility became increasingly impaired, they tensed up, leaning forward to the frosty windshield, then forced to drop back to a crawl behind a queue of lumber trucks.

The route home from Montreal was familiar to them from a lifetime of driving these scenic roads of the Laurentian Mountain, past Saint-Jerome and with Mont Tremblant somewhere beyond the blizzard's snowy curtain.

With all his might, Seymour clenched his Blazer's steering wheel. Milking the brakes, he maneuvered the four-wheel drive through gusts of blinding snow and ice patches.

He was seasoned in conditions on treacherous winter roads but on this night he had an ominous feeling in the pit of his stomach.

Maddie sat tight-lipped and checked her seat belt. Silence and fear had frozen their discussion of the Christmas family dinner and plans to attend the Warner's Christmas gala at Snowy Mountain.

White-knuckled and without blinking, Seymour tracked a pair of fading red tail lights. Further ahead the screeching and blaring of horns closed in around them as their vehicle careened head-on into a transport truck.

Seymour frantically spoke his wife's name as if he could somehow spare her the imminent tragedy. The lumber was tumbling and rolling toward them as the semi crumpled in around the SUV with seemingly endless horrific sounds.

"Maddie! Maddie!"

Among the attending emergency vehicles was a police cruiser, further ahead on its way to Lac Maurice. The band radio call and the description of the red Blazer shook Lieutenant Thorne and his accompanying officer. He dreaded traffic accidents on this perilous mountainous road, especially at Christmas. Too often the results were fatal.

By the time they arrived on the scene, it was apparent there were no survivors in the Blazer. The truck driver, dazed, was standing in the ditch, fumbling to light a cigarette in the blowing snow. He had crawled out of the cab window with only a cut over his eye and some scrapes on his face but was quick to deny his responsibility for a poorly loaded stake trailer.

"I know this family," Thorne muttered. "They have three children in Lac Maurice. This is tragic and so devastating."

Thorne and his accompanying officer departed before the coroner's vehicle arrived wanting to get to the Perkins house before any news of the accident filtered into town. The family was well-known and gossip would spread like wildfire.

Lieutenant Thorne would never forget that day, December 12, 1991. He pulled into the lane at Maple Drive and swallowed hard before taking the painful walk up the veranda. It was eight p.m. and the house was fully decked for Christmas. Thorne could hear chatter and laughter coming from the living room.

The eldest daughter, Polly, answered the door that fateful night. Her infectious smile disappeared in an instant.

A Year Later - December 1992

The bitter wind howled through the night leaving early morning snow packed in drifts up against the house, with the laneway tracks invisible. Lacey patterns of frost were etched on the window panes that hadn't yet given up their luster to the morning sun.

Polly was awake first and donned her favorite terry robe and headed to the kitchen. She had already made breakfast for Kate and Tim, her sister and brother, when they came downstairs. They relied on her as the assumed parent and breadwinner.

Gripping a strong coffee, she stood at the front window and ran her finger on the glass to draw shapes across the frost, then peered out at the morning drifts that gathered around the stately elms and spilled up onto the magnificent wrap-around veranda.

After a painful year of healing for the three of them, Polly had seen an improvement in her siblings and hoped the new Christmas would bring joy back to the household.

With her planned Christmas Day feast, she would fill the house with jubilant, happy guests, reminiscent of her childhood memories.

"Oh, I mostly long for the house to be full of love and laughter like it was two years ago."

For four generations, the Perkins family had volunteered in generous community roles to make the Christmas season magical for the children and families of even the poorest households in the quaint town of Lac Maurice.

The town itself rested in a fantasy setting, especially at Christmas, with blankets of snow settling over the hills of the Laurentian Mountains in the Eastern Townships of Quebec.

At the town's edge, the Perkins house had six bedrooms, one with an upper balcony. A parlor and banquet-sized dining room were off the front foyer, and a carriage house at the lane's end served as a guest suite.

The limestone estate was built by Polly's great-grandfather, Ichabod Perkins, as a wedding gift for his bride, and reflected his success as a prized art and antiquities collector. He was known to have scoured the countryside by horse and buggy to retrieve any morsel of history.

The antique hitching posts at the gate boasted elaborate wreaths and crimson bows as they had ever since it was the entrance to Ichabod Perkins inn, where weary travelers would rest and share a hot meal en route to Quebec City.

But the only community remembrance of Ichabod Perkins now was a brass plaque on a vintage post on Maple Drive that had once been the county road.

That post had been collected by Ichabod himself in Old Quebec City and had once tied up the horses outside Maison

Jacquet, past the St. Louis Gate, the revered house where Montcalm succumbed after the Battle on the Plains of Abraham.

Polly was born in this very house and it never occurred to her to sell the house when her parents tragically died last year. It housed a lifetime of memories and family.

The life insurance paid off the mortgage and household debts, and she was able to set aside a college fund for Tim and Kate. But the prospect of a nest egg for herself was not part of the equation. She couldn't remember life before Maple Drive and the sense of belonging to Lac Maurice.

The Weaver, Winslow, Freer, and Perkins families arrived in villages along the St. Lawrence as United Empire Loyalists and each generation served in the military as they embraced the French culture.

Seymour Perkins had been a fanatical historian dedicated to preserving local history through his antique shop, Treasure Box, on Sugarbush Street in Lac Maurice. Now the shop was the unexpected responsibility of Polly after her parents' accident. She found her predicament to be bittersweet as she was reminded every day of her father's absence but found solace in carrying on the family business.

Every Christmas, the streets of the town came alive with the festive French 'joie de vivre' spirit that had flourished for 350 years in Quebec.

The townsfolk were exuberant with the festive spirit, with main street horse and wagon sleigh rides, appearances by a local version of the Bonhomme snowman, and nightly bonfires at the skating rink in the church parking lot, serenaded by groups of carolers.

Bundled in a parka, Polly trudged out to start the Rover and chip the snow and ice from the windshield. At the turn of the key, the vehicle whined its displeasure, then the tires spun and squealed as snow and gravel spit out with no traction, wedged by a deepening rut.

"Polly! Polly!" She lowered the driver's window to see her neighbor rushing across with a shovel.

"Morning, Hank." She gritted her teeth to a grin. "Did my racket wake you up?"

"Naw, it's time for me to get to the shop. It's too much overnight snow for you to dig through, and I wouldn't be a good neighbor if I didn't give you a lift."

"The radio said the plows have cleared the range road. Tim and Kate have gone. They climbed through the drifts to get to the road and the school bus was on time."

"I see, and then the plows plugged up your lane with the extra," Hank chuckled. "What's that my Pa used to say? That no good deed goes unpunished? Now I understand."

The morning snowflakes were fluffy and light and melted on her shoulders as they fluttered from the sky. It was a relief to hitch a ride with Hank Moffatt into town to the garage where he worked as a mechanic. From there it was a five-minute walk to her shop.

"I'll drop you at the antique store, Polly."

"No need, Hank, I have my regular coffee stop on the way. They'd think of me as a missing person if I don't show my face."

"True enough. When times are difficult, there are still folks you can count on. Meet me back here at five, or if you don't show I'll come for you."

As the morning sun burned off the frost, the melting snow started trickling from the sidewalks to the curb. Polly trekked through the snow to the Treasure Box antique store, her shop—the very enterprise that two generations before her had cajoled and polished.

Traffic that dared the early roads skidded past abandoned cars and fender-benders, spurting muddy slush up onto pedestrians at the crosswalks.

As she walked, Polly gazed at the town hall's gingerbread house façade, then stopped at the life-sized nativity scene on the church lot. Across the street, banners flapped from the band shell's balconies. Like every December, the town was transformed into a Christmas fantasy land, with every wrought iron lamppost decked in greenery and oversized red ribbons.

Strings of white lights spanned Sugarbush Street, the main thoroughfare where The Treasure Box had been for years, and colored lights on the spruce trees reflected on the storefront glass.

"I'm blessed indeed with the peace and beauty of Lac Maurice."

The downtown merchants committee mandated Christmas decorations in the shops and windows, and a church choir sang carols on the boardwalk in the afternoons and twice on Saturdays and Sundays.

Townsfolk, out and about, dressed this month in elves' or Santa's hats and many wore gaudy Christmas sweaters to their places of work.

"The gaudier, the better," she laughed to herself.

A pickup eased beside her, and Carson Fergus called through the opened window. "Hello there, Polly. Want a lift?"

"Thanks, but it's half a block to the shop. Stay out of the ditches, Carson. I think the auto club will be busy 'til sundown!" She stepped to the curb and leaned in his passenger window to talk.

Carson, a middle-aged ex-fireman had always looked out for her since her Dad passed away. He'd been the best man at her parent's wedding and was considered family.

"Where's your car?"

"I couldn't get it out of the drive. Hank will be by tonight and I'm sure he'll dig us out with Tim's help."

"If he doesn't, Polly, you give me a call."

"I sure will, Carson." She patted the passenger door and he pulled away as she waved.

At Sal's Coffee Bar, the overhead bell jingled as Polly lifted her head to the aroma of freshly baked bread. Brushing snow from her boots on the welcome mat, she shuddered to shake off the chill.

"Ah, sure smells good!"

She unraveled her scarf and let her jacket slump the chair, relieved at being unbundled from the cold.

Even after a snowstorm, the café drew its crowd of faithful locals, there for the warm morning pastries and baking, the ambiance and the comfort of daily laughter and chatter with friends.

Sal's décor and nostalgic fifties ambiance was a novelty in town, with black and white polished floor tiles, and vintage chrome stools and chairs with seat covers in red vinyl.

After fifty years, the original emporium had closed its doors, but Peggy, a long-time employee, saw the chance and reopened the bakery.

Barely inside, Polly spotted her matronly friend at the counter. "Morning, Peg. What's hot out of the oven?"

"Sunshine muffins today, dear. I'll get a plate with a side of butter, and you'll want coffee to thaw out. Your face is frozen."

Polly pinched her cheeks. "Yes, my skin is frosty, Peggy, but I'm mostly exhausted and hungry. On a day like this, no one will be inconvenienced if I open the antique shop a few minutes late. Other than shopkeepers and your loyal bakery customers, no one is foolish enough to endure today's sidewalks."

"My helper, Charlie, will be along soon and he'll shovel my front sidewalk. Can I send him to do yours too?"

"That'd be great, but I insist on paying Charlie his customer rate plus a nice tip."

"He'll not object to that."

The hostess wiped her hands on her apron and brought Polly's muffin and mug to a window-side table.

"Also, Peg, a box of sugar cookies for my customers."

"Right, I'll bring them over. I just have a table or two to attend to."

Peg's head motioned to look over her shoulder at the women encamped at a corner booth. "Every town needs women like those. They're arranging the Christmas Bazaar and Tea at the Church for Thursday afternoon. I'm not much for organizing committees but I have a penchant for hand-made crafts and sweets."

"Thursday . . . I'll make sure I can go. I always did that one with Mom."

Cradling the mug in both hands, Polly blew away the steam and artistically dribbled the cream onto the surface, watching it form an imaginary shape of tiny clouds that slowly dispersed and vanished below. At this moment, all seemed right in the world.

Behind her, the doorbell jangled and she listened to the familiar voice of one of the town's policemen.

"Hey there, Peg," it boomed out. "Can you fix up two hungry blokes?"

"Sure, Wayne. You know I can do that."

"I'll have your breakfast sandwich and a blueberry muffin. Can you warm it?

Peg nodded with a thumbs up and turned to his partner.

"Jackson, what about you?"

"I'll keep it simple," he said with a smirk. "Just double his order and add a tall black coffee."

Wayne called out to Polly by the window. "Coincidence seeing you today as my wife will be by your shop any day now. She found a box of old books and photos in the attic that you might want to look through. They date back to your mother's ancestors—the Winslows."

"That's my passion, Wayne. Old things." She laughed at the sound of her words. "I'm always looking for new stock."

She stopped as her eyes fell on Wayne's partner, Jackson Tripp.

His appearance was striking—tall with a strong jaw, thick dark hair and an unusual color in his warm eyes, brown, mixed with green.

From the outset, Polly felt a personal connection with Jackson, and it now seemed strengthened whenever their eyes met.

After Montreal police academy, Jackson Tripp moved back to his childhood roots in Lac Maurice a few years back, partnering with Wayne Crawford, a senior patrol officer.

Peggy was watching Polly's reaction and couldn't resist a chance for matchmaking on her friend's behalf.

"The annual Policeman's Christmas Ball is going to be a grand event. Is your wife looking forward to it, Wayne?"

"Always . . . and every year it costs me a new dress."

"What about you, Jackson?"

"Yes, I have tickets."

"And . . ."

Jackson turned away with a blush. "You are quite the inquisitive sort, aren't you, Peggy? If you're asking about my date, I prefer to keep that to myself for now."

"Sorry . . . that was prying. Jackson, your coffee is on the house."

Polly avoided embarrassment with a last sip of coffee and gathered her coat and bags. "I have to get to the store, Peg. I'm ten minutes late already. Send Charlie along when it's convenient."

"It was nice seeing you, Polly Perkins," Wayne said.

Polly and Jackson exchanged an instant glance, and as he tipped his hat her smile broadened and she was out the door.

Mrs. Warner's regal stature and the shiny black sedan waiting by the curb announced her arrival. Standing outside the antique store, she made a point of looking at her watch with a visible huff as Polly approached.

She was a grand matriarch of Lac Maurice, from the row of estates over on Prospect Hill. Her luxurious, wide-brimmed feather hats and those of her competitive cronies kept the millinery shop on Acorn Street in business.

"I'm sorry, Mrs. Warner. I didn't know anyone would be along in this weather."

"Weather, schmether. It's punctuality that gets you along in life. It would do you well to ponder the American idiom 'you're a day late and a dollar short'."

"That's practical and wise. My father taught me to be on time and I apologize. Come in and make yourself comfortable as I light the Tiffanys. My car got stuck, and I'm not used to the outdoor chores my father always did."

The matriarch softened at the mention of Mr. Perkins.

"I suppose that is a consideration . . . I'm sorry if I appeared a bit short at the door."

"Not at all, Mrs. Warner. Is there something special we can do for you this morning?"

Mrs. Warner was a stately eighty-year-old, still standing five foot seven and erect, with a silver bouffant of upswept hair. This morning she wore a vintage wool hat with a curled brim and woodcock feathers.

She sat in a tapestry-covered side chair as she picked and pulled at each gloved finger to free them one at a time. Sharp in wit and mind, she normally enjoyed a good tangle.

Over the years when Mr. Perkins had received an antique shipment from Britain with silver tea serving sets, he always invited Mrs. Warner to come and review them first. Critiquing fine antiques would be her priority for any day.

"I'm hosting a Christmas party at the manor," she said. "I need two pairs of stately candelabra, tall and standing high, with five arms if possible. I'm not sure what's going on these days, but I suspect my staff has pilfered a few of the silver items. I haven't had anyone really reliable since Meredith Carver. You remember her, don't you? I think she was a Hanson."

"Meredith Carver . . . oh yes, she was always meticulous and with the best manners. I know it's hard to maintain suitable employees. If I come across any of your monogrammed silver, I'd be sure to advise you."

Polly thought for a moment. "I do have some unique silver candelabra. Would you mind if I look for them and get them polished up? You could come back in a day or two, or I could send them to your house for your approval."

"Thank you, Miss Perkins. That will be fine. I'll get Withers to bring me back tomorrow afternoon."

"You know you can always call me Polly. Father always spoke so highly of you, I feel like I've known you all my life. He always talked about the grand lady from Snowy Mountain that comes into the store. He said you had a keen eye to select the finest treasures, besides your wit and charm."

"That is sweet of you, dear, but I do like to keep up the pretenses."

Mrs. Warner's old, pale aquamarine eyes twinkled with pleasure as she was turning to butter at Polly's gracious handling of the situation.

"Your father was a dear man, I really was drawn to him in our youth." Biting her lip, Mrs. Warner wished to take back her words. "Excuse me, but when I said that it was just an old lady chattering and nothing of course untoward."

Polly gave a reassuring smile to ease her client's blush.

"Before you go, Mrs. Warner, have a browse through the shelves and I'll put on the kettle if you'd like a cup of tea."

"Yes, I'd like that. Withers won't be expecting me for another few minutes."

Polly was enjoying the game and brought out her mother's favorite Limoges cups and saucers, the ones with black and baby blue diamond pattern. She took her greatest care to have everything exact, with the silver sugar tongs, fresh cream, and the polished silver tray.

Mrs. Warner puttered through the store making a selection of several items from the china cabinets.

"Polly, these are perfect for the Christmas event. We're having a lot of old friends, you know the stuffy codgers and their gassy wives. But if you'd like, I'd be happy for a sprig of fresh air if you'd like to attend. Of course, bring a gentleman guest."

On the mahogany counter, Polly methodically wrapped each item in tissue. "That is very kind of you. I would be delighted to attend. My parents always looked forward to the party at your estate as the best of the season."

Mrs. Warner reached with her now gloved hand to touch Polly's arm and allowed a twinkle in her eye.

"Yes, dear. You might just be the belle of the ball. I'm glad we had this little chat."

Inside, Polly was giddy with excitement that she tried not to show. It was beyond a dream in town for anyone to be invited just once to the Warner's Christmas Ball, to be able to hobnob with the most prominent society members from Montreal and Quebec, then even written in society columns with photos and tidbits of celebrities and Who's Who.

Flashing back to her childhood, she recalled standing on Sugarbush Street on a Saturday evening as the glistening ebony carriages passed in the direction of the Christmas Ball.

For an instant, she closed her eyes to imagine the sound of the clomping hooves of sleek fine horses marching past toward the black iron gates of the estate at Snowy Mountain on Prospect Hill. The driver wore a black tuxedo and top hat with green and gold garland gracing the carriage as he jingled a leather strap of brass bells.

As a child, she opened her hands to catch one of the candy canes tossed to the children watching on Sugarbush. It was a grand magical parade.

The kettle whistled in the back room, and she jumped up for it. In her brief daydream, she'd almost forgotten that Mrs. Warner was still there, waiting in the tapestry chair for tea while rattling on about various townsfolk who had attended the soirées in the past.

"This is indeed an honor for me, Mrs. Warner. I was reliving some memories."

After spontaneous chatter about childhood and her family, the doorbell jingled as Warner's chauffeur, Withers, presented himself to collect his boss.

"Thank you, Polly. This was a delight today and we'll be back tomorrow afternoon as you suggested."

"My pleasure. And Mr. Withers, Sir . . . there are several packages."

Charlie was already clearing the snow and sprinkling sand on the steps and walk. "Miss Perkins, Peggy sent me. I hope the snowbank is fine at the curb, as there's no other place for all this snow. I made a bit of a trench for the water run-off as the snow melts."

"It's perfect, Charlie. In fact, anytime it snows, I'll be happy to pay you well for your service."

From her handbag, she drew out a few bills, watching his eyes and face for a smile to know how much he expected.

"That's generous, Miss Perkins. I'll come whenever it snows or ices up – it's important to keep the melting off the sidewalk so no one falls."

Polly watched through the window as he skipped down the steps with a grin, whistling as he packed his wallet away.

In her head, she imagined her father's voice the last time they were together in the shop—'From now on Polly, you're in charge of window displays.'

She looked at the grandfather clock ticking loudly in the corner of the room. "Sophia will be along soon to help me. Another half hour."

She unpacked a postal shipment, tossing aside the bubble wrap and crumpled paper. On the counter, she laid out an exquisite hand-carved nativity set, then three more.

"One of these is for the window display, for Dad."

On the tapestry settee, she sipped her tea and sighed with relief.

"It will be good for business for me to socialize … but a gentleman guest!"

2

"It's not that I'm unattractive. I'm only twenty-four, and I'm told my golden brown hair and blue eyes are my best features. But I'm not ready for a smothering relationship again. Bryan was too protective and I can't encourage him even in the slightest way."

Days before, Polly got wind of local gossip that Bryan was ready to propose to her in a surprise public announcement at the posh country club at Butler's Corners.

In a panic, she summoned Bryan and abruptly broke off the acquaintance, insisting she'd never actually been his girlfriend or even that they were a courting couple.

She reflected back now on the words she used to end it.

"Sorry, Bryan," she had explained. "I fear I have misled you and I do apologize. You know how rumors get around town, especially from the idle conversation at the Country

Club, and in this case, they spread to town faster than you realized. I've always thought of you as my good friend, but not in a romantic way."

With his shaky lip showing a visible sudden dejection, she moved quickly to recover his feelings.

"But those same rumors also abound at the hair salon on Maurice Gate. I heard Mrs. Gaines the last time I was there, discussing her daughter, Laureen, who has her heart set on you, Bryan. Perhaps you should give her a chance since she is already half-way there. Don't worry, I'll let the word out that you dumped me."

Parting with a handshake, she heard within a week that Bryan and Laureen were seen dining at Colonel Butler's Steakhouse.

"Ah, I did some good matchmaking."

As Polly smirked about her diplomacy, the bell over the door rang, startling her.

"Sophia! I'm glad you're here."

Sophia was a single mother of two. Her strong French accent with its slight edge would distinguish her in any crowd. At thirty-five, she displayed a nonstop glowing personality, with a merry, round face that showed off her disposition. She was always the first to laugh at anything the least bit amusing.

Her arrival was a relief to Polly at this moment of deep thought as she was a confidante on many matters.

"Bonjour, Polly . . . you've got a bit of a mischievous look on your face. You don't need to wait until I've got my coat off to start telling me."

Polly burst out a laugh.

"You're more than perceptive. It's uncanny, Sophia."

The two knew how and when to boost the other's spirits. Although ten years Polly's senior, Sophia held a respectful admiration for her boss that was invigorated by their kindred sisterhood.

"It's awfully quiet in here. What's going on anyway?"

Polly rambled on about being late for Mrs. Warner and her request for candelabra, waiting for the right moment to tell Sophia about the ball.

Patient for Polly's reply, Sophia went about setting the stereo with a selection of Christmas carols to pipe through the outside speakers.

"That's better," Polly said. "I've been preoccupied with a conundrum. Mrs. Warner invited me to the Ball."

"Wow! You're so deserving, and I'm so proud!"

"Sophia, I need a gentleman guest."

The two were silent as it digested.

"A gentleman guest! I see. Don't worry, Polly. This will be easy to solve. If the bachelors in town knew you were available, they'd be lined up at the door. And double that if they could escort you to Warner's Ball."

"Ha! I'm not sure about that."

"If I may be so bold as to make a suggestion?" Sophia ventured.

"Be bold, please. I need that."

"At the coffee shop when those policemen come in, the quiet one, Jackson, always sneaks a look at you. He has those adorable, brown puppy dog eyes. You must have noticed."

The two stared at each other as Polly's blush faded to a smile.

"That's nonsense, Sophia. Jackson Tripp! He's never even given me the time of day."

"Don't you think he's rather handsome?"

Her mind flashed back to Sal's that morning when she looked at him and her heart stopped momentarily.

I wonder when that started.

"I'm certain Jackson has a girlfriend. He as much said he had a date for the Policeman's Ball."

"Who is it?"

"Well, he didn't say exactly."

"Just give it a little thought, okay?"

The warm blush seeped back into her cheeks and she retreated to the back storeroom in her father's dust apron to delve into the boxed inventory.

"Without a doubt, I remember seeing candelabra. I can't disappoint Mrs. Warner, it's unthinkable."

Time got away from her as she sorted antiques. Her passion, since a child, was to dig through items that offered a glimpse into history . . . old pictures, inscriptions in books, jewelry, and family albums. An hour later, she surfaced with two dusty boxes filled with some hopeful silver candelabra and a collection of forgotten gems for the shop.

"Here, Soph, we need to polish these up for Mrs. Warner. These are so elegant. I can envision the occasions in past generations and families when they would have made a table splendid."

Polly held up a magnificent silver twist-stem with five arms, each dipping and then rising to a regal height.

"This one is going to be the apple of Mrs. Warner's eye. She won't find another like it outside Montreal."

Polly folded her arms and stood back, admiring each piece as it might have stood on a grand table back in the 19th century. She tilted her head to one side, as her father would have teased.

"I should have lived a hundred years ago, then these would be polished every day," she joked.

The snowplow had finally cleared Sugarbush Street, leaving high snowbanks and an icy surface, a hazard as tires spun and skidded at the intersection.

At the blast of horns outside the shop, they both scrambled to the window to witness screeching, then the thud and crash of metal at the corner of Sugarbush and Geneva.

"Sophia, call 911."

Polly slipped on loose galoshes and raced through the snowbank to free a young woman pinned in an old Honda, with the radiator cracked, and steam hissing from the hood. The driver was stunned and confused but with no signs of serious injury.

In seconds, Wayne's cruiser pulled up to the crowd of curious locals bunched at the curb, and he jumped out to attend to the driver.

From the other side, Jackson went first to the check on the pickup, then quickly to Polly who was consoling the woman.

"I'll take her statement, Wayne," he said. "The truck is from the utility company and the driver says he's okay. They'll send their insurance investigator, and EMS will check him over."

Jackson leaned into the Honda. "Are you alright, miss?" The driver was about Polly's age. She had a disarming head of what Polly thought to be luscious carrot curls and false eyelashes. The young woman feigned dizziness when she saw the handsome officer.

"I'll need your help to get out," she pined, but Jackson seemed oblivious to the woman's interest in him. Polly saw it right away.

"No, you have to stay put until EMS gives the green light for you to be moved in case you have an injury that's not immediately noticeable."

The driver closed her eyes and flipped her head back deliberately flirting with the officer.

"Polly, did you see this happen?" Jackson asked.

Sophia's description of his big, brown puppy dog eyes flashed in Polly's memory, and she felt her tongue twisting.

"My shop is right there. The snow is so high we couldn't see it, but we heard the squealing of tires before the crash."

Jackson was now looking directly into her blue eyes and she felt weak. "Thanks," he said in a kind voice. "I'll come by later for a statement."

"Come to my store. Here's my card with my number."

Irked by the competition, the woman snapped, "Excuse me, Officer. I'm the victim, not her."

In a fit of drama, she then warbled, "Please help me now. I feel too weak."

"I see you're busy enough here," Polly said. "I'll get back to the shop. It was very nice seeing you, Jackson." On the way back, she wondered if she'd been too forward.

Curious townsfolk popped into the store through the day hoping for crash updates, and Polly took advantage of the traffic, selling extra wreaths and nativity crèches. She played Sophia's favorite French carols, *O Peuple Fidèle,* and *Les Anges Dans Nos Campagnes,* in the background and kept a pot of Christmas spice tea on the go, with trays of Sal's sugar cookies to encourage shoppers to linger and chatter.

Over and over, Sophia relayed the tale of the crash to customers, with excitement in her voice for the crowd, and Polly began to echo the same effervescent pitch.

"You should have seen it," Sophia embellished to a growing audience. "The two vehicles were coming from opposite directions. We heard the squeal of brakes, then the thunderous impact of crunching metal."

She raised her hands into the air with a sudden clap. Earlier in the day, she realized the visual and dramatic sound effects captivated her customers as they lingered longer over the merchandise.

"Boom! Boom! The sirens and firetruck were instantaneous, but thank goodness there were no serious injuries. Officers Wayne and Jackson were so skillful in taking matters into hand."

One of the town gossipers, Mrs. Church, was all ears. "It must have been frightening for you girls."

Looking across, she saw Polly and went to approach her. "Polly Perkins, aren't you Bryan Gilford's girlfriend? I heard there was news of wedding bells on the horizon."

"Me! Oh no, you are mistaken. I went to high school with Bryan, but we were just acquaintances. You must be thinking of someone else."

Polly enjoyed the disappointment on the gossiper's face.

"I was sure . . ."

"Mrs. Church, it certainly wasn't me, but I heard in the hair salon that Bryan had been seen at Colonel Butler's Steakhouse with Laureen Gaines. Mrs. Gilford was in the same salon the other day, raving about what a lovely girl Laureen was. They would make a lovely pair, don't you think?"

Mrs. Church juggled the juicy news. "I must be on my way now. Thank you, Polly—I have a phone call to make, then a ladies lunch where we always have plenty to share."

Polly sighed with satisfaction that Mrs. Church would quickly dispel the gossip at the church tea.

By one o'clock, the shoppers had dwindled, allowing a reprieve to restock the shelves of wreaths, hand-made stockings, and holly-scented Christmas votive candles.

The hustle and bustle of customers continued throughout the morning, and Polly was grateful for an early afternoon reprieve to re-stock again.

At each tinkling of the customer bell over the door, Polly instinctively turned to look. When Officer Tripp finally arrived in the afternoon, she was busy with a customer and didn't notice as he waited.

"Hello, Jackson. I didn't expect to see you again so soon. Do you have more questions for me?"

"I was back taking measurements at the scene and thought I'd stop and see if you are alright."

The sight of the handsome policeman in the store turned customer heads in curiosity and started a buzz of whispers.

"Oh, yes. It's actually been good for business," she said.

"I've heard. I picked up coffee at Sal's, and Mrs. Church was upset that your engagement to Bryan Gilford is off."

"Engagement? We were high school friends but never like that. The town ladies fantasize to create a bit of fun, and it seems I was the bane of their joke. I told Mrs. Church that Bryan has been wining and dining the Gaines girl . . . a tidbit keeps the gossip chain from collapsing."

"I know what you mean. Whenever I'm at Sal's, someone tries to match me up. Wayne's no help either, he's all for it.

I guess it's the consequence of a small town. The relentless matchmaking."

They both laughed at the painful circumstances, then she looked into his greenish, warm brown eyes, feeling like the world had unexpectedly slowed to a crawl.

The front door burst open, with Cynthia Crawford carrying a box wrapped in old brown paper and tied on all sides with burlap string.

"Hello, Polly! Wayne said he told you I'd be by."

Jackson stepped over to help. "Oh, excuse me, Mrs. Crawford. Let me assist with that." He was every bit a gentleman, the kind that still holds doors open for any lady.

"Please, Jackson."

He plunked the box on the counter, and with Polly otherwise occupied, he made his excuses and tipped his hat. Their eyes connected again. "I'll stop by again, Polly."

Cynthia was slow to notice their prolonged glance, then suddenly the dots connected. "Oh. He was here to see you. Wait 'til Wayne hears about this!"

"Cynthia, don't tell Wayne. Surely you remember those embarrassing days when the town's busybodies tried to match up everyone single?"

"How dreadful it was. Thanks for reminding me. You're safe—Wayne will never know."

"How's your mom, Cynthia?"

"Her health is fine, but I had to get out of the house as she has taken over my kitchen completely. The Gingerbread House contest at the town hall has her possessed. Icing and gumdrops are everywhere but the kids are loving it."

From the counter, Sophia burst out at the image. "Cynthia, enjoy it while she's still spirited and able."

Polly's vision escaped to her own grandmother at the old Winslow house, then her mother's kitchen at Maple Drive, and she longed to be back there.

Sophia jumped in, "I'll put in my vote for your mother's gingerbread, Cynthia. Didn't she get last year's blue ribbon?"

With a fake grimace, she said, "As a matter of fact, yes, and now it's mounted in a frame in the darn kitchen. Nevertheless, your votes would be awesome."

Polly untied the string and folded the brown paper wrap. "And what's here?" She thumbed into the open box.

"It's real vintage stuff from back in the Winslow era. I peeked inside and wrapped it up again. Your mother was a Winslow, wasn't she, Polly?"

"My mother's mother was actually a Weaver, and she married Franklin Winslow. I'd forgotten that your house belonged to our family back then."

"Seems no one thought to clear out the attic since. I just poked enough to figure out it didn't belong to us."

"Ooo, yes! I'll be eager to pilfer into these documents. I love delving into old things about history and genealogy. I'm so grateful."

"Well, mostly I hope these tidbits will bring you joy this season, Polly."

"Stay for a cup of Christmas spice tea and Peg's sugar cookies?"

Cynthia removed her coat. "Lovely. Christmas spice is on my list. Twinnings will have a new shipment today. Mom can't get through Christmas without it . . . cinnamon, apple, cloves, orange. Then there's mulled wine on Christmas Eve with raisins and cinnamon sticks. It's magical, she says."

"I saw the billing outside on the lamppost for Thursday's Bazaar at Rev. Dennison's Church," Sophia said. "That's where Bill and I got married and both my kids were christened. I've never missed their tea even once. Oops, Polly, can you spare me some minutes off Thursday for it?"

"You know I will, Sophia. Will your mother have other baking?"

"We already have two dozen Christmas cakes in the kitchen, ready for the almond paste. I'll pick up plastic green holly bits with red berries today for the tops."

"Your mom can put two cakes aside for me, as I'm not sure if I'll make it Thursday."

3

Polly's fingers nimbly ran across the tops of the folded parchments, aged documents, and cardboard photos from the last century. A sensation of euphoria enveloped her as she organized diaries, certificates, pictures, and tin plate negatives into piles.

"This is incredible. My mother once told me a fascinating tale of mystery back in the Winslow family. There are very few Winslows left now from that line, and the daughters moved away."

Sophia peered into the box, then at Polly's face. "I see the new pleasure in your expression already. If there's a story to be told in these documents, I know you'll find it."

"I'll leave it here until I get my car back. It's the sort of treasure to muddle through at home by the fireplace."

"I must go, Polly. The kids will be home from school." Sophia grabbed her red parka from the coat rack and headed for the door.

She turned back. "Maybe you should show Jackson a spark of encouragement."

With a blush, Polly perked up. "You think so?"

"I don't think he came to make measurements. He was without his partner and came to see you . . . yes, you. He has the potential to be your gentleman guest."

"Get on your way, you old soothsayer."

Half an hour later, she was hanging a 'closed' card in the window when Polly saw Hank pull in front. He tooted, and she poked her head out.

"I promised you a lift home, Polly!"

"Five minutes and I'll be ready."

On the way, Hank chattered incessantly about each event of the day. "You wouldn't believe the fender-benders and cars in ditches. The tow truck's been running all day and a night crew will finish up. There was even an incident in front of your shop."

"Oh yes. I saw it."

"When I got there," Hank said, "the gal in the Honda didn't have a scratch on her but was persistent to ask about the police officer. I pretended I thought she meant Wayne, so I said he was married with children. Wouldn't want to waste a good bachelor on a scam artist."

She giggled at his mischief, but it hit closer than he knew. "I'm sure Jackson can make his decisions in that regard."

Hank maneuvered the ice-packed ruts on Maple and honked at Tim who was digging the snowbank blocking the lane. He was the image of his father, tall with squared shoulders, high cheekbones and a shake of freckles across the bridge of his nose.

"Hop in, Tim. With my plow, I'll take care of this."

"You're a great neighbor, Hank," Polly said as she traded places with Tim. "Thanks."

For a demure fourteen-year-old, Polly's sister Kate was already competent with her mother's old Watkins blue rag recipe book. Her hair was dark like the Weavers. Tall and lanky, she'd already overtaken Polly in height.

"Hey, Polly! I'm making Mom's Onion Meatloaf, mashed potatoes, and green bean casserole. Hope you're hungry."

"I'm ravenous, in fact. The aroma got me at the door."

"By the way, Pol, there's a message for you by the phone. Some guy."

"A guy?"

Kate winked. "And he sounded pretty good."

Still in her coat and boots, her curiosity took her directly to the message.

"Ah . . . Jackson Tripp."

"He said he'll see you at Sal's in the morning."

"I didn't give him my home phone number, Kate, but my card from the store. Not that anyone is hard to get a hold of in a small town." She shook her head. "It seems everyone knows everyone else's business."

I wonder what this is about.

Twenty minutes later, Tim burst into the side kitchen door, leaving a dollop of snow from his boots.

"There better be supper on the table!" he declared, then the three siblings burst into instant laughter at his mimicking the sound and words of his father every evening when he arrived home, meant to tease their mother.

"Thanks for clearing the snowbank," Kate said. "Sit in Dad's chair and I'll dish you up an old-fashioned supper." She sat a jar of her mother's green onion chutney within his reach.

"Mmm . . . meatloaf!"

"The town is buzzing today with Christmas spirit," Polly said. "You guys interested in volunteering? Our family has always sorted food hampers at the church, and Reverend Dennison needs help for the lights and music boards for Saturday's pageant. Tim, he asked about you, with your experience."

"Busy, busy, busy, aren't we?" Kate shrugged. "I'll pitch in with the food hampers. Mother would want that."

"Great. Can you call Mrs. Brant? There's a message by the phone."

"I'll call the Reverend," Tim groaned. "I like doing the tech booth on Sundays. Does that get you off the hook?"

"Oh, no. There's always more," Polly said. "I'll work the rental booth for skating tomorrow night, and I'll sew some costumes tonight for the pageant."

"Shepherds again?" Kate asked.

"Wise Men now. It seems their outfits have gone awry again this year. I think the kids take home the gold braided tassels for their personal collections and don't return them."

Tim tipped the chair back on its heels and pretended to tuck his fingers into suspenders, mimicking his father.

"The Perkins family does it again!"

In the morning the roads had been plowed by the township and were clear. Polly dropped Kate and Tim at the

Louis de Buade Frontenac high school, then sped off to Sal's to arrive before Jackson.

"Good morning, Peg."

"You're here early, Polly. What's up?"

"Yesterday I was late opening, and Mrs. Warner was waiting outside my shop in a bit of a huff. So I allowed ample time today. I calmed her down with a cup of tea and your sugar cookies. I'll take some gingerbread men today if you have them. It's a boost to business."

"Of course, I have them. Do you mind if they're out of the freezer? They'll thaw in twenty minutes. Today's are still in the oven."

"No-one will complain. They're always devoured on the spot."

"Polly, are you going to the tree lighting at the band shell tomorrow night?"

"We have every year as long as I can remember. Everyone in town turns up and we hang around with hot chocolate and marshmallows by the bonfire. And you?"

"How could I not? I have the hot chocolate wagon. Cliff and Monique will have to help as I'm doing double-duty in the church choir. I had to learn *O Tannenbaum* in the French version. It's *Mon Beau Sapin*, and *Little Father Christmas* is *Petit Papa Noel*. I hope you'll be there to hear that." They both laughed.

The bell over the door echoed throughout the café and Polly's heart jumped into her throat. When she thought it was safe, she turned her head quickly, hoping for Jackson.

It was Lois, from the dress shop two doors down. "Morning, Peggy. Two mediums with double cream to go. Oh, hello, Polly. How's your Christmas business?"

"Up from last year, thankfully."

"Mine too. A lot more tourists are in town this year." Lois added two cranberry lemon slices and was out the door.

"I'll take a slice of that too," Polly said.

Taking off her coat, she slipped into yesterday's chair by the window. Her eyes fell to her watch discreetly as she knew she only had about ten minutes.

"You expecting someone, Polly?"

With an exaggerated, fake grit of the teeth, she leaned into Peggy. "Are you taking over for my Mom?"

"Somebody has to."

Their incessant cackle was suddenly silenced by the bell and Wayne's booming voice from the door. Polly's head tilted and her nerves jumped.

"Where's your sidekick today, Wayne?" Peggy asked.

"He'll be right in. He's ticketing a car double-parked."

"Whose car this time?"

His head shook. "Does everyone in town have to know everything? A rental, maybe—I didn't recognize it. There are more strangers around now. A tourist bus here from Ottawa has taken over Peabody's Inn and old Quebec loaned us their Bonhomme snowman. The council promotes us as a Christmas town and most rooms at the inns and hotels are full. Ha, ha! Get that? The rooms at the inn are full?"

"Catchy," Polly mocked. "I'll remember that."

From the window, Peggy was still glued to the ticketing outside. "It's the red-headed girl from the collision. What company in town rents Corollas to someone that was just in an accident?"

"Everyone knows Carson Fergus has the only rental agency but he rarely has any cars available," Wayne said. "It'll be a dead end but I'll check to please you."

They all turned as the door opened.

"You all watching me?" Jackson asked. "I gave her a warning."

"A warning?" Peg said. "That's all she deserved?"

"She saw me writing the ticket and rushed from the ladies store for pleading me to stop. The poor girl was the same one from yesterday—her name's Bethany. She asked me to coffee, but I said that would be a bribe."

He looked at the three of them, but his eyes settled on Polly. "I can't take bribes, of course."

Moving to her table, he removed his hat. "Can I sit with you for a minute?"

Her eyes sparkled. "Sure. I'd enjoy the company as long as you don't consider it a bribe." The rest of the café fell silent waiting to see what was about to happen, especially Peg and Wayne.

"No joking. This is important, at least to me." Jackson paused and looked at her as if he'd first met her. "The Policeman's Ball—I'd be honored if you would be my date."

Polly felt the red flush rising from her neck up into her cheeks. From across the room, she sensed the inquisitive eyes of Wayne and Peggy.

"Yes, Jackson, I'd like that. But I have a request as well."

Jackson sat back and lowered his voice. "I'm puzzled. I didn't expect that kind of reply."

"You see, I received an invitation to Warner's Ball on Christmas Eve." She tilted her head. "And I need to bring a gentleman guest."

He sat back, expressionless. "So is this a deal or a date?"

Without a smile, his face was hard to read, and Polly wondered if he'd been offended.

"I would prefer that it's a date."

"Then it is. I'll be honored to be your gentleman guest."

He stood, but his gaze lingered before he stepped up to the bakery counter. Flustered, Polly gathered her belongings. She'd always thought of herself as being in command of her emotions, but this new warm feeling was disarming.

"Don't forget the gingerbread, Pol," Peggy called.

To reach the cakebox, Polly brushed Jackson's sleeve and detected a scent of after-shave. With a long blink, she recorded this as she hadn't been near a man in a year.

Jackson reached for the box and lowered it to her hands. The warmth of his brown-green eyes connected and she knew this was the moment when it ignited her soul.

Perhaps this is someone I could let into my life.

Polly's hand was shaking as she fumbled with the key in her store's lock, and in slow motion, she turned the brass doorknob.

Stepping inside, she saw the store in a different way, as if for the first time. The pine threshold that sagged in the middle had always been that way, the same worn flooring that had born a lifetime of her father's weight. There, behind the counter, was her father, a genial, white-haired, smiling gentleman of sixty years. He beamed at the sight of her.

"No, this isn't a ghost, Dad. I can see you. You're here right where you always are," Polly whispered.

It was a magical, nostalgic moment, as she imagined his familiar voice. Her eyes glossed as she gazed at the hardwood floorboards that still shone from under his worn shoes.

"I love this place . . . the jingle of the bell and the creak of the heavy door when it opens."

She breathed in the beeswax smell of the antique store. "I'm so secure here."

Her memory of Seymour Perkins, her dad, was at times bigger than life, not just of cherished family times, but of his love for history and his precious antiques. At a moment's notice, he could tell a tale to captivate any imagination, stories of Quebec and from his studies of explorers like Cartier and Champlain and the native lore of the Wendake and Oka.

It wasn't a passing fancy for Polly. The love of historical antiquities began with Grandpa Perkins who himself told tales of his own grandfather who fought in the Fenian Raids.

Her eyes scanned every nook and cranny trying to associate memories as she went. Then a thought struck her.

"By gosh, I'd forgotten about that old post office desk in the dining room."

Polly was compelled to a roll-top desk that her father had often used while in the store and made her promise that she would never sell it.

She could practically hear Seymour's voice. 'It must stay in the family, Polly. Something you need to always remember is to cherish the past and preserve history.'

Fingering the crevices, she carefully opened each drawer. There was a batch of sales bills from the 50's, a ring of old skeleton keys, some ringed receipt books of store expenses, and a cluster of envelopes.

As she picked up the envelopes, she could see that the bottom of the last drawer was different—there was a knob. When she pulled on it, the bottom of the drawer rose like a lid. Below was a small secret drawer with more documents.

The hourly gong on the clock shelf jolted Polly back to the reality of the premature passing of her parents. She listened as the chime echoed to the ceilings of the emporium.

"Oh, Dad, why did you and Mom have to be on that bend of the road when the lumber truck was barreled through, and with Christmas trees no less? If time could be changed by seconds, you would still be here with me. It's hard to have Christmas without you."

It was little comfort that her parents hadn't suffered as their lives were snatched away. The truck driver had only minor scrapes and a fine, without as much as a remorseful apology to the family for their loss.

Today, December 12th, was the anniversary. The memory and pain were still fresh to her, of a pair of officers delivering the unthinkable news. Their condolences were sincere, but grief became a process that no one could predict, with last Christmas becoming a season of funerals and estate dealings.

The stereo perked her up. "This Christmas is different; I have hope. Perhaps it's with Jackson Tripp."

She flashed back thirty minutes to Sal's. "I'm sure I made a mess of that. I'll just pick up and get over it."

With shopping traffic building, she hauled her fixtures out to the sidewalk, with a barrel of festive twigs and willow wreaths with holly berries, a basket of antique drawer pulls, and a stack of horse-hair welcome mats with Christmas ink inscriptions and etchings of Bon Noël.

Beside the door, she hung stockings on an ornate stand, intertwined with antique bells.

I wish Mom were here for advice what to wear to a ball. She was gorgeous at formal events. Surely there'll be something in her closet.

4

From a window step ladder, Polly surveyed the merchants' storefronts up and down Sugarbush. Everett Forrest, sweeping outside his barber shop, waved hello from across the street and motioned to see him. She locked the door and scurried over.

"I'll spare only a minute, Everett. Your barber pole is a work of art with the garland and tinsel twisted around the barber stripes. From my store I see so many kids stopping to pick candy canes that you hang across the window. That's so generous."

"Not just kids," he roared. "All ages come for the treats and I replenish them every day. Here's a cane for you, Polly, and an extra for Sophia. In this season, folks are friendliest, and more charitable—everyone drops change in the Sally Ann kettle over here.

At the plug, the Santa kettle keeper boomed, "Ho, ho, ho, and a Merry Christmas."

"You know, it's not the season that brings the town joy. The folks do it . . . folks like you, Everett. I must go as Sophia doesn't start till noon."

"Bless you, dear girl. Now run along."

While Polly was alone in the morning's idle time at the Treasure Box, she dusted one of the old leather-bound diaries from the box under the counter. She let her fingers run around the etched initials on the front corner—M.H.W.

"Diary of Millicent Henrietta Weaver. That's my Grandmother Winslow. I wish I could remember her better."

Inside was a loose black and white photo of a stately, young woman. Her hair was in an upsweep, and she stood tall in a frilly dress, with a cameo at her neck.

Slowly, imagining that her mother was there to listen, Polly read aloud.

"December 12, 1938. Dear Diary, life has been complicated lately. My heart aches as I sit here with you, my only true friend. Father insists that I attend Warner's Ball with Franklin Winslow, but my heart yearns for Jeremiah Hanson. He is tall with the most unusual eyes. They're sparkly brown with an odd emerald hue. It was a portal into a beautiful soul. He is the perfect gentleman and walked me home last night. When I am beside him, I have an odd, rambunctious feeling in my chest and tingling in my toes. I longed for him to kiss me but that would be against the rules . . ."

Polly's heart was pounding, enough that she didn't hear Sophia come into the store.

"Gracious, girl! Where have you been?" Sophia declared.

"Why? Do I look peculiar?

"Definitely absent, like you've been away in another world."

"In a way, you're right, Sophia. I was reading an old diary and I was captivated by the romance of a bygone era."

Sophia edged closer. "Can I read it?"

Polly closed it quickly. "Sophia, I would be betraying a confidence to share it. This is very personal and has been a secret of my grandmother for many years. You understand how private diaries can be."

"I'm sorry. Of course, I understand."

"But I do have big news for you. Jackson Tripp asked me to the Policeman's Ball . . . and I got the nerve to ask him to Warner's Ball."

"Fantastic, when . . . ?"

"At Sal's, before work. Sophia, I realize that I really do like him."

Sophia clenched her hands. "I knew it," she gushed.

"Now serious stuff. Can I wear the same dress twice or do I need two?"

Still absorbing it all, Sophia giggled. "Oh, absolutely two."

"Would it be pitiful if they're from Mother's boudoir?"

"Your mom was a looker for sure and always dressed impeccably. That's okay for the old folks' ball at Warner's. But for the Policeman's Ball—definitely something new and slinky."

"I knew you'd give it to me straight," Polly teased. "And . . . old folk's ball?" The two cackled at the words.

"That reminds me, Mrs. Warner is due this afternoon."

"I'll polish and display the candlesticks on the table right under the crystal chandelier. That lighting will make the silver glow and highlight the attributes of each candelabra."

"Mrs. Warner will be impressed with these choices."

At exactly two, Mrs. Warner swung open the door, jingling the bell, followed closely by the uniformed Withers. Her eyes went directly to the table.

"Oh, gracious, dear, are these the ones for me to see? They're as magnificent as you said, and the right height."

"I'm so glad. We can both envision the grand affairs and galas where these very silver candle holders have shone."

Polly touched each one as she spoke and peered closely as if saying goodbye to a friend. "Many folks no longer appreciate the delicate artistry of these silver rosettes entwined on the curved branches."

"Yes, it's so true, dear. If all your antiques could talk, we'd never leave this delightful shop."

Mrs. Warner's voice had become softer and sweeter, and at the table's end, she gathered four of the largest five-arm candelabras.

"Will you have tea while we box these up for you?" Polly offered.

"Very kind of you, dear, but we have a list of errands this afternoon, Withers and I."

Mrs. Warner suddenly rooted through her handbag. "I have an invitation here for you, Polly."

"I am very grateful for your kindness, Mrs. Warner."

Polly's eyes glassed up at the calligraphy inscription on the vellum crested envelope—Miss Pollyanna Perkins and Guest.

"It's my absolute pleasure, dear. Something about you reminds me of my granddaughter . . . like you're a kindred spirit."

"That is a grand compliment, Mrs. Warner."

Something about the comment unnerved her, and after Mrs. Warner departed, she needed a breath of fresh air.

"Sophia, hold down the fort—I'm going to Tiffany's Designs to check out dresses. It's nagging at me, so I might as well deal with it."

"If I may suggest then, something slinky in black, and don't forget sparkling stilettos and a striking clutch."

"Sorry, Sophia, you can't come," Polly laughed.

She pulled her sweater tight over her chest and disappeared out without a coat. The echo of the door slamming behind her brought a smile.

The air was crisp, but Tiffany's was only half a block down Sugarbush, in an area of eighteenth-century houses converted to upper apartments over shops. Below the quaint balconies and French dormers, many stores displayed plaques of the history and original owners.

Tiffany's brass nameplate read:

Abraham Godham residence built in 1815. Col. Godham fought under General Montcalm at the Battle of Abraham in 1812. He took the opportunity of a land claim offered to the British military for services and bought a double claim at Lac Maurice before it was a town. Mrs. Godham established the first apothecary shop in all of the Laurentians saving many lives during the Fenian Raids.

"I must search the history of the Perkins land and verify their military service. Cynthia said she sent a box of old medals to the museum. However, answers about the Winslows may already be in my treasure box of diaries."

A crowd of shoppers was on the curb to cheer the approach of the Mayor's jalopy, touring the district. From the open back seat, he called out through a blow horn.

"Merry Christmas, one and all. Remember Lac Maurice's tree lighting Saturday evening! Come one, come all!"

As he passed, he raised himself up and waved straps of jingling horse bells to the audience, and in return, they roared back their delight. A lad walking in front masquerading as an old-time town crier rang his handbell, with his soprano voice announcing the tree lighting ceremony.

At the dress shop, she dallied outside Tiffany's luxurious window display, studying every gown and accessory, with each mannequin draped in black and silver.

"Good afternoon, Polly," Mrs. Slater called from the back while steaming a new outfit. "You'll be needing a party dress, I do believe."

"What do you mean?" Polly bristled gently. "Do you have recent news about my entertainment schedule?"

"Just small talk, Polly. I picked up coffee at Sal's, and Peg confided that you've been invited to the Policeman's Ball."

"Preposterous! Is nothing confidential in this town?" Polly bit her tongue but she knew she'd already let her tone become edgy.

"Dear Polly, be assured it was in strict confidence. Your secret is safe with me."

"Thank you, Mrs. Slater, I like to keep my life private. You understand."

"Certainly, Polly." Mrs. Slater was glad to close the discussion. "Now, I saw you looking at the window displays. Is there something that caught your eye?"

"Sophia says it should be black and slinky. One in the window seems to fit the bill."

"I know the one you mean, and indeed Sophia is right—black and slinky. And I assure you no one will know what you bought."

"I'd like a guarantee with that." Polly looked Mrs. Slater straight in the eye. Although gossip was part of town life in Lac Maurice, a person's word was valued and trusted as well.

"You have my word, Polly."

"Then I'll try that one on, please."

"I have one on the rack in your size."

Mrs. Slater drew down a wooden hanger draped with a fine silk black sheath with long sleeves. It was snug-fitting with a properly scooped neck to show a bit of cleavage while maintaining enough sophistication.

Polly stood at the change room mirror admiring herself as she turned a full circle. Mrs. Slater tapped at the door to break her trance.

"Polly, I have a delightful sequined clutch and patent shoes to go with that. Jackson is a good six-feet tall and the heels would be quite flattering."

She gasped at the first sight of Polly. "It's absolutely splendid. The dress was made for you."

"It does feel good, but shouldn't I try on something else for comparison?"

"You know the answer." Her face beamed with revived enthusiasm. "I have plenty more that would suit you."

Mrs. Slater hummed as she sorted hangers. "This silver and pearl swathe skirt is also elegant. Does it appeal to you?"

"I wouldn't personally have chosen it off the rack, but I'll try it. My mother's costume diamond necklace might even work with it."

She critiqued it privately in the change room, feeling the weight was heavy because of the beading. But it was oddly familiar.

I know what it is. Mother has a similar dress in her closet, perhaps that's the one for Mrs. Warner's Ball, and the black one for Jackson's party.

With her decision, Polly exited the dressing room without demonstrating it for Mrs. Slater.

"The black one without question, Mrs. Slater, and the accessories too. You have such an eye for design."

With the flattery, Mrs. Slater changed her tone. "Oh, Polly, I do my best to keep customers happy. I understand about the gossip and I promise no one will even know you were here."

"You're a dear, Mrs. Slater, my mother always bought her fancy dresses here and appreciated your confidences."

"Bless her soul."

"Thank you. Mom often reminded me how confidences and trust are a two-way street. She swore me to secrecy about Mr. Tupton."

Polly took silent pleasure at the moment, watching the startled look on the shopkeeper's face as she realized Polly knew a sensitive bit of gossip about herself.

"Be assured, Polly, my lips are sealed." Mrs. Slater said with a shaky voice.

Polly was almost at her Treasure Box antique shop when an official-looking black sedan pulled up with a crest on the side of the car—Argenteuil Township. A nondescript man in a long grey coat and black fedora got out and entered.

With heightened curiosity, she picked up her pace and reached the door behind him as his monotone voice was addressing Sophia.

"I'm looking for a Pollyanna Perkins. I have information that this is her place of employment."

"I'm Polly Perkins, Sir."

The gray coat turned slowly to face her. "May I have a word with you in private, Miss?"

"Come this way."

She led the visitor into a side room where antiques were displayed but with no customers in earshot.

"I'm Milton Marlborough from the county seat. I represent the Land Divisions office, in particular. We also work closely with Legal and Risk Management in Montreal."

"What's this about, Mr. Marlborough?"

"It has come to our attention that your parents passed away untimely last year. I'm certain that they left adequate life insurance for you and your brother and sister. Although the mortgage was cleared by an attorney in Montreal, we have received a historical claim against your land."

Polly's mouth was open and she was unable to speak.

"Who? What?"

"A claim dates back to the marriage of your great-grandmother, Millicent Weaver, her marriage to Franklin Winslow. You may not be aware of the circumstances but your grandmother's family owned the Winslow house and we've followed the land transfers of that property. Millicent had two children: Madeleine and Stanley Harris.

"Unfortunately, Harris Winslow, the son of Stanley Harris has made a claim that the land you now live on is rightfully his. The son had a record of legal disputes with the family as a young adult and took action at that time to disown any affiliation with them.

"But his legal counsel now argues that Harris should have been kept in the original will and would have inherited the property."

"Impossible. This is all wrong and I can prove it."

"That's not for me to decide. A date for Discovery is set for the first week in January. I didn't want to bring this to you before Christmas, but in fairness, you need time to prepare."

Milton Marlborough laid a dossier on the table and tipped his hat.

"Here is a copy of the claim."

He was gone before Polly said anything.

5

Aghast yet fervent to delve into the mystery, Polly left the shop in Sophia's hands with the Winslow box secured under her arm. After dinner, she sat by the fireplace ready to face whatever it held for her.

Preoccupied with the Winslow mystery, she avoided Kate lest her anxiety be apparent.

Dear Box, I hope you have answers that will let us keep our house. Surely there are deeds and agreements in these documents to prove Mom and Dad are rightful heirs.

Kate bounded in the front door from school. When Polly was home she always eagerly greeted her siblings so Kate became curious about his sister's distraction.

Sitting down on the floor in front of the fireplace, she was unaware of the troubling legal news and Polly's urgency to pour through the box.

"Kate, this diary is from December 1938. It's written by Grandmother Winslow, revealing her innermost secrets to us. You wouldn't remember her as she had passed away before you were born, but she was magnificent and Mom's mother."

"I don't remember hearing too much about her, do you?"

"Let's see. I've seen a family Bible that says Grandmother and Grandfather Winslow got married in 1939 just after the beginning of the Second World War. This diary entry is from the year before that."

Kate curled her feet under her as Polly started reading aloud.

"December 16, 1938, Jeremiah received his conscription papers this morning. I can't bear the thought of him going overseas to fight the Germans. He says it is his moral responsibility to serve and protect his country, but I can't find it in my heart to agree. It is an amazing love where our souls are united into one. The world can spin as long as it likes as long as I can stay in the arms of my true love. He'll be shipping out on Saturday. My parents and the Winslows think they have made a match with me and Franklin, but I could never love Franklin as I love Jeremiah. I am expected to sit with Franklin Winslow and his family at church on Sunday. I'm being deceitful, dear diary, please pray for me."

"Who is this Jeremiah?"

"It seems Jeremiah Hanson was Grandmother's first love. I don't know much about him. Perhaps the diary will explain," Polly said.

"I never thought of old people in a romantic way," Kate muttered. "Is this her picture? She's beautiful." The photo was faded and they held it to the lamp. "Did Grandfather Winslow fight in the war too?"

"Yes, he did. I believe it was from 1939 to 1944 when the war ended on Armistice Day."

"What happened next in the diary?" Kate asked. "I can't believe we're seeing her own words. Read more."

"December 17, 1938. Mrs. Winslow has invited me to dinner Saturday night. How can I go the very day I say goodbye to Jeremiah. I know she is pushing poor Franklin to give me an engagement ring for Christmas, but I don't love him like I love Jeremiah. P.S. Jeremiah kissed me behind the barn tonight, it made my toes tingle.

December 18, 1938. I am so happy tonight. Jeremiah and I pledged our love to each other and he asked me to wait for him. I don't know how to tell Father and Mother, they have their hearts set on me marrying Franklin. I loved being in his arms, so strong and caring and it was a blissful union stamping our love forever. I am a new woman, his woman."

"I'm now getting the gist of what's going on. Poor Grandfather Winslow," Kate mused.

"By the way, Polly, did you see that Jackson fellow today?"

"I was going to tell you. He is tall and handsome as you know, Kate, but most of all kind and gentle. Folks say he's shy, but I'm sure it's attributed to respect."

"Your eyes twinkled when you said that."

They both giggled. "I do like him. He invited me to the Policeman's Ball next Saturday in Quebec City."

"Oooh, that's fancy."

"I bought a dress at Tiffany's today for Jackson's party. It's black and slinky. But he'll also come with me to Mrs. Warner's Ball. As she's older and stately, I thought you might help me look through Mom's dresses for something regal. I want to wear her diamond necklace."

"Mom would be pleased about that. It's good to talk about our parents and memories. It's been a tough year, and I don't often thank you for looking after us."

Polly slid over beside her younger sister for a hug.

"You really give us love and a stable home," Kate said.

"Enough of that, Kate. I was hoping to have a grand feast here on Christmas Day like it was when Mom and Dad were here. What do you think?"

"I'm all for it. I can wash and iron the linens right away, and polish the glasses and silver. It will be like Mom is here with us. Thanks, Polly. Who will you invite?" Kate winked.

"Mrs. Warner's Ball is on Christmas Eve, and I don't want to smother Jackson with invitations and scare him away."

"He wouldn't have invited you if he didn't like you a lot. You should be able to find out his Christmas plans without being pushy."

"Is there anyone special you'd like to invite, Kate?"

"No boyfriends, Polly, but there's a misfit girl at school, Monica. Her parents died so she's like me in a way, as she lives with her grandmother. I've become a bit of a substitute sister since not many of the kids hang with her. We could invite them both."

"That's very thoughtful, Kate. Let's do that."

The chatter came to a halt at Tim's huff as he strode through the front hall.

"What's the matter, Tim?"

"I missed an assignment and was forced to sit through detention. That's why I'm late."

Polly was on her feet to console her brother. "A plate of pork chops is in the oven. Sit at the dining room table and get some food into you, then we'll talk about how we can help with the assignment."

"Tim, I can help!" Kate volunteered.

He looked at them woefully. "After supper, can I get a lift to the library? I can get the essay done there. I know you want to help, but I'll get Price and Louise to meet me—they are in my class and have the same problem."

"Okay," Polly said. "I'll take you when you're ready and pick you up when the library closes."

"I'll walk Louise home, so don't worry. I'll get here on my own."

Kate and Polly exchanged a glance and a subtle nod.

At midnight, Polly tip-toed in the upstairs hall to make sure Tim was in his room. She was relieved but wide-awake and went directly to the old Winslow box in the living room.

"December 19, 1938. Franklin is upset with me. Betsy McLuhan told him she'd seen me with Jeremiah behind the barn. He blamed me for embarrassing him and his family and called me a name that I won't even tell you, dear diary. My situation is even worse now. Jeremiah leaves tomorrow and I agreed to be intimate with him as our farewell love gesture. I consider us to parallel the tragedy of Romeo and Juliet. He is my only true love. I won't spell it out for you, you know what I am saying."

There was no entry for the next week.

"December 26, 1938. Dear diary, it's been a terrible few days. I'll never forgive Betsy McLuhan for what she's done. Everyone has turned against me except dear Franklin. He's been a complete gentleman when I confessed my affections of the heart were elsewhere. Jeremiah had only been gone a short time when he was trapped in a German ambush in Normandy and his body and soul are torn from me. My heart is broken, I feel that I can bear no more. My heart breaks every night and I long to be with him. Except something unusual is happening to my body. I am both delirious with happiness and devastated with the responsibilities in store. My true love has left me with a sacred gift."

Tears streamed down Polly's cheeks, carrying a burden for Millicent Weaver's heartache. From the living room window, she watched the moonlight that cast across the fields, then at the light snow flurries wafting from the sky.

"Nature is so beautiful. I wonder what Millicent saw that night when she looked out the window. No doubt she'd be remembering their last gaze . . . perhaps his brown and emerald eyes speaking a romantic embrace with his eyes."

Her thoughts turned to Jackson. "Why is it I feel this affinity to Jackson when I read Millicent's letters?"

Sipping on a cup of tea, she read on.

"January 7, 1939. Dear diary, the unbelievable has happened. I need you now more than ever. Mother says I must see the doctor tomorrow. I was frightened to tell her but she's been very supportive and hasn't judged me. I've been rather peaked the last few days. I'm sure it's a touch of flu but I feel depressed and can't eat."

"January 10, 1939. Father is furious and Franklin is so kind-hearted I don't feel I deserve his devotion. He knows that the child belongs to Jeremiah and persists that we should marry right away. My family will never forgive me for the shame of what I have done, yet I am glad for what Jeremiah and I had together. Be patient with me, dear diary."

Polly thumbed through another batch of papers and found the wedding certificate of Millicent Henrietta Weaver and Franklin Theodore Winslow, dated January 24, 1939, at the Bonaventure Baptist Church in Montreal.

Notations in the diary dwindled until August of that year when Millicent announced the birth of their daughter, Madeleine Fairchild Winslow.

"July 27, 1939. Dear diary, she is the most beautiful child ever. Dear Maddie is a total delight, smiley and sparkling sky blue eyes with a bit of emerald green. We have moved into the Weaver-Winslow mansion on Cricklecreek Road. It's a beautiful house and we have an apartment of our own with a nanny hired by Franklin's mother."

"Maddie was my mother. I never knew this about her parentage. So she never really had Winslow blood, but rather Hanson and Weaver blood. Madeleine was born exactly on time, not six weeks premature, according to Millicent's confessions." She rubbed her tired eyes ready to give sleep another chance.

Morning came too soon, and Polly awoke to a clatter of dishes and the smell of bacon.

"Kate, is that you in the kitchen?"

"Who else would it be?"

"Bacon and eggs? It's not the weekend yet, is it?"

"No, silly, it's Friday. What's the matter with me making you breakfast on a weekday?" Kate teased.

Tim rounded the corner too. "Bacon . . . mmm. The smell just reached my room."

Polly took her usual chair. "Listen, guys, tomorrow night is the tree lighting at the band shell. I'm going, are you?"

"I'll be there," Tim said, "but I'll get there on my own. I've invited Louise."

"That's fine, Tim. You don't have to account to me for anything. I'm not trying to replace Mom and Dad, just keeping this family together."

His nod gave her assurance. "I know that," he said.

"But I'll come with you, Polly," Kate piped.

"If we go early, we'll grab a bite at the Midway Diner. Tim, did you get that assignment done last night?"

"Everything is cool!"

Polly skipped her regular coffee stop at Sal's, irked that it was the source of gossip bits about her life and Jackson. Instead, she went to Peter's Deli for a take-out coffee and a bagel with cream cheese. It was a fast food place without tables or any reason to linger, and she immediately realized she missed Peg and others.

Continuing the walk toward her shop, she passed Sal's and waved at the window, relieved that the local police cruiser was not outside. Barely past, she heard her name.

"Polly, wait up!"

"Hi, Jackson. I didn't mean to be rude not coming in."

"No problem. In fact, I'm glad to run into you without an audience." She rolled her eyes at the predicament.

"Would you go to the tree lighting with me tomorrow?"

Polly stumbled for the right words. "I really would like that . . . are you aware of my family circumstances?"

"I'm not sure. I know where you live and that you lost your parents last year. Do you mean something else?"

Polly appreciated his sensitivity. "I promised supper to my fourteen-year-old sister, Kate, at the Midway and to go to the tree lighting with her."

Jackson's eyes fell but bounced back instantly. "Polly, would it be terrible if I took you both to the Midway then to the band shell? Feel free to say no, and I'll understand."

"Jackson, that is so sweet. I couldn't say no to that."

"I'll look forward to seeing Kate again too. Is five okay to pick you up?"

"You've met my sister before?"

"Sure, a couple times. We're called to the school at times. She witnessed some bullying last month ago and I took a statement from her. She is confident and knows who she is."

"True. She's a lot like my Father."

As he nodded, she again looked into his sparkling, warm brown eyes.

I see how Grandmother must have felt looking into Jeremiah's eyes.

"I'm so sorry for what happened to your parents, Polly."

He reached for her hand and she held tight. "Thanks, Jackson, for being so understanding." She glanced at Sal's window down the street and hugged him anyway.

Polly generally took Friday afternoons off, and for the Christmas rush, she arranged for Mrs. Bentley, a long-term part-time employee, to come in to help Sophia with antiques.

I'll plan an evening next week with the girls as a holiday gesture, perhaps Colonel Butler's Steakhouse or the new French chef Jacques Bedoes on Sumac.

When Sophia arrived at noon, Polly was in gear to tackle an afternoon of Christmas shopping and groceries.

"Hey, Sophia. When Mrs. B. gets here, pick an evening out for us girls. It's time to do our wine and dine."

As Polly stepped onto the sidewalk, she paid no heed to a silver Saab rounding the corner onto the main street. The driver appeared to be searching for something and slowed in front of the Treasure Box. When he saw Polly, he sped up and disappeared at the Sugarbush and Acorn intersection.

6

The silence at her heritage house struck Polly as she entered, and she wondered why she hadn't heard it so deafening before.

Have the floors always creaked like this? I never noticed that the slightest sound echoes, especially the ticking of the grandfather clock. I wish the walls could talk. I have so many questions.

With the legal urgency of Harris Winslow's claim, there was no time to waste, and she went directly to the documents box and sat cross-legged on the floor to find more answers.

On the floor, she placed eight small diaries beside a stack of legal documents tied with heavy black ribbons. Beside them was a scrapbook of marriage and birth certificates as far back as Montague Weaver.

Returning to Millicent's diary of 1941, she came across an important statement then searched the documents and scrapbook for a corresponding validation.

"May 15, 1941. Dear diary, I have no one to talk to. Franklin is devoted to me, but he sincerely wants to have a son, a son of his own. So far, God has not seen fit to allow me to become pregnant again. Several times, I have brought up the consideration of adopting a child who doesn't have loving parents of his own. Mother Winslow strongly objects but in time she will see that's the only way. Please give me strength and pray that Mother Winslow drops her objection.

"September 2, 1941. Thank you, dear diary, for your prayers. Franklin and I have just returned from Quebec City where we completed our application for a dear two-year-old boy, named Stanley. This will be the answer to Franklin's prayers . . . his own son and a sibling for Maddie."

Searching for validation in the documents, Polly found a piece of paper showing Stanley Winslow's birth parentage of an unwed mother from Nova Scotia and the date he was officially adopted that year. Another adoption paper was in the file for Harris Winslow, son of Stanley Winslow, who was adopted 25 years later.

Ah, interesting. Here's a land transfer title giving the Weaver-Winslow property to Mom after Grandpa passed away with a reference to a Codicil bequest to Stanley Harris, the half-brother. What else?

Returning the documents to the box, a parchment letter fell to the floor.

Clearly, Stanley Harris was given assets and investments equal to the value of the Winslow house years ago, then allowed to remain in the house with his wife and son until it was sold to the Crawfords. Why would his heir want to make a claim for the Winslow house now?"

Clipped together were more documents related to Harris Winslow. Stanley Winslow made an appeal to Maddie and Seymour Perkins to pay for Harris's university education since he had burned through his inheritance. The Perkins obliged but insisted on a final paper to absolve the family of any further financial obligation.

I'll forward anything relevant to Milton Marlborough to object to the claim filed against us.

Kate burst in through the front door. "Friday at last!" she shouted and flung her backpack down the hall.

"I have news, Kate. Jackson wants to take us both for dinner and the band shell tree lighting Saturday."

Kate stretched her legs out on the sofa. "Polly, I won't be a third wheel, if you don't mind."

"Don't think that. If you're uncomfortable I can cancel with Jackson."

"No way. I was keeping you company but I'll go with Monica to the tree thing as she needs to get out and meet people. But I'm still on for supper with you and Jackson. So are you inviting him for our Christmas feast?"

"Kate, I'd like to but we are just casual acquaintances stuck with each other for reasons of convenience."

"We'll see about that. There are plenty of single women in Lac Maurice that your eligible bachelor could latch onto, yet he chose you. I heard Peg say once that you have to remember to get on the bus when it stops at your corner, otherwise, you've missed it!"

"She's said that to me a time or two. I'll take a day at a time."

Polly's Saturday morning blueberry pancakes and sausages were ready for her siblings, and she tapped on Kate's door. "Honey, I have some errands to do. I'll be home by noon. Mumble 'okay' that you heard me."

"Ok."

"Breakfast is in the kitchen. See you at five."

With notes from the document box, Polly arrived at eight at the library and was directed to Census and Land Records to search the Winslow name. Settling at a research table, she started with archive files from the Lac Maurice Express.

The wedding announcement of 1939 for Millicent and Franklin Winslow was easily found; then the obituary of Jeremiah Hanson in December 1938 as killed in action.

Next, according to township records, the house on Cricklecreek was deeded to daughter Maddie, who sold the house to the Crawfords at the time of her marriage to Seymour Perkins.

In a worn leather book by the Argenteuil Historical Society, Polly thumbed through pages of land divisions since the arrival of the United Empire Loyalists, finding more genealogical records of the Perkins and Hanson families.

Ancestors of Jeremiah Hanson had fled to Quebec after the American Civil war, among the fortunate that amassed portable wealth in the United States that they fled up the Ohio Valley into Canada. The Hanson family bought land surrounding the village that became Lac Maurice. The first settlement at Hanson Ridge was long forgotten beyond the interest of the Historical Society.

So there are Hanson descendants other than my mother. I wonder what happened to Wilhelmina. It's all gobbly-gook! I wish Dad were here to help me make sense of all this.

As shapes of library patrons moved about in the stacks, Polly stayed engrossed in research, unaware of time. Close to noon, her trance was broken as Myrna Sutcliffe took a seat at the study table.

Myrna whispered, "Hi Polly! Are you researching?" She raised a large reference book, *Pioneers of Lac Maurice*.

"We have a history club that meets once a month. We're always looking for new members, especially descendants of our old pioneers. Are you interested in joining?"

Polly whispered, "I've got to go now, but let me know when you meet next and I might come if I can."

"Who are you looking for, Polly? I might be able to help."

"I need that, Myrna. Next time, could you help me find out more about the Winslow and Weaver families? And the Hansons too."

"I know this library intimately, especially this section. You're asking the right person. I'll pull some files and give you a call."

On the way to her car, Polly got waylaid in the quaint shops on the side streets and drawn to the hardware store that had converted to its annual Christmas wonderland.

An outside speaker piped music over the sidewalk, and a cluster of children pressed their faces to the window, transfixed by the animated display of Santa's sleigh mounting onto the roof of a miniature house. In a scene from *The Night before Christmas*, the tiny reindeer's prancing hooves moved back and forth creating a childish fantasy.

Santa Claus is Coming to Town was playing over and over, and she stepped through the big door into the transformed, magical emporium, leaving her problems of the Hansons, Winslows and Lac Maurice outside.

I remember the first time we brought Timmy here. He was so enthralled that he sat fixed in the corner on one of the crates and refused to leave. Those were the days when children believed in fairies, elves, and Santa Claus.

A miniature steam train puffed a cloud of smoke as it circled the white powdered terrain. In a flashback, she recalled Tim's tiny voice as a boy. "It's coming, it's coming!"

He'd rise on his tiptoes each time the trains climbed the hills and crossed the bridges through the mountain tunnels. My sweet memories.

Nearby, a small wide-eyed boy tugged at Lydia Fergus's coat. "This is the best day of my life. I could watch this all day, Mom."

Polly sidled over with a grin. "It's a wonderful place, isn't it, Lydia. Every child should spend an hour in here, whether young or old"

"You're so right. Carson pretends he brings the boys here for their amusement, but I know he just becomes one of them when he's here.

At the joy of this moment, and in the spirit, she was overtaken by an urge to set up a moving train in her Treasure Box shop window.

"Imagine the young and old bundled outside in the falling snow, then stepping inside where my shop is already brimming with fantasies. Our lighted miniature villages will blend in, and Tim can help me."

It got better as she thought it out, and on a mission, she found a clerk she recognized, dressed as an elf, named Dan.

"Can you help me? I want enough track, trains, and landscape for my window."

"Gosh, I'd love that, Mrs. Perkins."

"Dan, I'm Polly . . . Tim's sister. You were in his primary class at Champlain Elementary."

"Sure," he said, disoriented "Do you have a budget?"

As Dan packed her parcels in the trunk, she turned to see what other shops might inspire her and caught a glimpse of Jackson and Wayne almost a block away, talking to a young woman.

"Bethany again, she's like a bad apple that keeps popping up from the bottom of the barrel." Polly instantly regretted her sarcasm that rebuked the ingrained sense of charity and kindness her parents imposed. "She didn't do anything to deserve that."

Moving to the curb for a clearer view, she watched as Wayne stepped away, then Bethany moved in close to Jackson, wriggling her arm into the crook of his elbow. Polly felt an undeniable surge of jealousy.

"No point in being the wounded bird, but when he asked me to the Policeman's Ball, he was clear it was a date. I'm not sure what to do about this territorial attitude I'm experiencing."

Polly marched toward Sal's. "Peg cheers me up and I could use a coffee."

On the way, she popped into Fiske's Jewelers for Christmas pins with rubies and emeralds for Sophia and Edith, then returned them to the trunk, wrapped with gold and red.

Sal's lunch rush was over and Polly instinctively pitched in to help clear tables.

"Hey, girl, it's your day off," Peg bellowed from the kitchen.

"I can't leave a mess alone." With a damp rag and Lysol, she polished an empty table.

"I didn't say to quit doing it, Pol, just that it's your day off." The pair laughed.

"I'm glad you're here today, Peg. It's one of those times when I'd like a chat with my mother."

"Oh, darling, what's the matter?"

"I'm like a school girl with a crush on the handsome guy on the football team, but the cheerleader keeps showing up to flirt and manipulate."

"Have a chair, love. Have you had lunch today?"

"No, I've been on the go since I left the house early."

"Charlie makes the best beef stew on Saturdays. It's the only time I let him cook, but the customers ask for it so it's a regular thing now. I'm bringing you a bowl and a calming tea. It's what your mother would have done."

When the last table had cleared, the two women took their favorite corner booth.

"I know you pretty good, kid. I've watched you grow up with skinned knees and braces. You come from good stock and the way you were raised will get you through. You've got the spit and fight of your father, and the gentle charm and delicate heart of your mother. That is a compliment."

"Thanks, Peg."

"My kids are off to college but I'm capable of seeing young love. You've been so busy with the shop and raising your brother and sister, and you haven't listened to your intuition."

"About what?"

"Your heart."

"I haven't wanted to date anyone. It's too complicated."

"Don't make a conclusion without allowing the facts to present themselves, dear. The ball's only a week away. Be your mother's girl and let the gentle charm and delicate heart have its way."

"I'm annoyed for becoming jealous."

"I should tell you . . . Wayne and Jackson were in this morning for their usual. Jackson always asks if you've been in and he watches everyone that passes the window. I know he's looking for you. He's a good man. His family has lived in the area for close to two hundred years, not that it's relevant in being a match for you, but give him a chance."

"On my way here, he was talking to the girl from the accident. Whenever I see her, she's flirting with him. I don't want to make a fool of myself, but I feel that he's mine . . . at least for now."

"See, dear, you said it. Now be yourself—that's what appeals to Jackson—and don't worry about floozies. He's not that kind of guy."

"Thanks, Peg. You're right about conclusions. That's the same advice Mom would have given me."

Polly felt that a weight had been lifted. She'd been bottled up about the Winslow claim and driving home, she became excited about seeing Jackson at the diner in a few hours.

The house was quiet and she found two notes by the phone. The first message was that Kate would be a few minutes late meeting Polly and Jackson at the diner.

The second was from Tim. 'I'm having supper at Louise's house. If I don't see you tonight, Polly, remember I love you.'

"Why would he say that?" Troubled, she checked his room. Nothing was out of order, but a nagging feeling sent her to the master bedroom that had been left untouched since her parent's passing. Everything had been left as it was that fateful morning, just waiting for Maddie and Seymour's return.

She froze. Her father's top bureau drawer was open. "The watch case is empty. Grandfather's pocket watch!"

Polly pulled on a cashmere red sweater and primped her hair to wear under a knitted hat. The weather report for the tree lighting suggested flurries and dropping temperatures later that night. In her mind was the worry about Tim.

The Midway Diner was on Cumberland, a block south of Sugarbush. It was a 50's diner with table jukeboxes and waitresses with short yellow aprons, frilly caps, and pencils behind the ears and tinsel corsages. The front had the shape of a subway, with the window ensconced with chrome and a neon signature.

Jackson was outside waiting, standing at attention like a soldier to be inspected. His eyes were fixed on her slight shape as she approached him. She wasn't sure if she should shake his hand or lean in for a hug but he solved it and put his arms around her.

She blushed and their eyes connected. "Polly, I know you well enough to see something's wrong."

Polly smiled demurely. "Have you volunteered to be my genie in a bottle and give me three wishes?"

"I'm game to give it a try."

Jackson led her to a red, vinyl cushioned booth by the window, paying no mind to the whispers and prying eyes at other tables.

"Is Kate still coming?"

"Yes. I'm sorry, I should have told you right away. She left a note at home that she'd be a few minutes late."

"Then I will gladly sit with you on one side and we'll leave the other for Kate."

"Do you have siblings at home, Jackson?"

"I don't live at home. I have a basement apartment at Wayne's. You know the old Winslow house on Cricklecreek Road? My parents lived in the country near Hanson Ridge and I have a brother that moved to Montreal."

"Of course, I know the old Winslow house. Well in fact—my mother's mother was a Winslow."

Jackson was stunned by the revelation. "Well, I didn't expect that."

"Remember when Wayne told me Cynthia had an old box for me? That's what it was about?"

"I never made the connection."

"It's my nature and I can't help it. I'm a history buff and love to solve a challenge. If you're interested sometime, I'll show you what I found."

A waitress, Flora, interrupted with a tray of ice water. "What can I get you folks to drink?"

"I've had too much coffee. But a ginger ale, please."

"And a Coke."

Flora motioned to the bench. "Is someone else coming?"

"Yes, one more, any minute."

Like clockwork, the door opened and Kate rushed in. "Polly, sorry I'm late—I'll explain it later." Her eyes went to Jackson.

"I'm Jackson Tripp. We talked once at the high school."

On the spot, Kate presented a refreshing, new air of confidence. "Of course, the officer. I didn't recognize you in street clothes."

Amidst their chatter and small talk, Flora brought their platters of the daily special: Salisbury steak with mushrooms and gravy, seasoned fries and a side of coleslaw.

"Looks yum!" Kate blurted. "Pol, you remember that I'm going to the tree ceremony with Monica, right?"

"Yes, I know. By the way, did you see Tim this morning?"

Kate's face tightened. "I thought he left you a message."

"He did, but it just leaves more questions."

"I'm sorry, I'm not my brother's keeper. You should ask him later."

Polly nodded, knowing Kate wouldn't be a stool pigeon. Embarrassed by the interaction, she quickly turned the subject.

"Jackson, at the hardware store today, I fell in love with the lights and sounds of a magical Christmas train display. I couldn't help myself and now I have a trunk full of landscape and trains to lay in my shop window. Maybe I can hire assistance from a professional?"

"I'd love to do it, Polly. Perhaps Tim too."

Kate had few words as she ate, and in no time was ready to depart. "Thanks for supper, Pol; and Jackson, it was nice to see you again."

In a flash, her black ponytail and blue parka were out the door.

7

"It seems you have a lot on your mind. I'm a good listener if you like."

Polly saw the sincerity in his eyes. "I do need someone to talk to, Jackson. You are just too generous and I don't want to ruin things."

"True friendships are built on trust and understanding. Whenever you are ready to talk, tell me."

Her throat choked up and she whispered to get the words out, "I know that." She felt like she was falling softly from a cloud and a safety net was waiting to catch her.

Walking across the park, Jackson's hand brushed hers and their hands intertwined.

"Polly, sometimes a boy like Tim just needs another man to talk to . . . just a friendly suggestion. I'm afraid I've been in that situation and I understand all too clearly."

"You are a dear and intuitive man, Jackson. It's difficult to be a parent and a sister in the same stroke with a fourteen and seventeen-year-old. It's especially hard with Tim as he's testing his independence. He misses my Dad and I don't lay down rules for him, fearing a blow-up. I had no warning to prepare or get advice from my parents on how to deal with younger siblings."

"I'm not a stranger, Polly. I've known your parents since I was a kid and I've always kept my eye on you. You won't remember, but I was your newspaper boy when you were in primary school."

Polly's face flushed red. "Gosh, is that really so? You've kept your eye on me over the years?"

Jackson looked flustered. "You were a few years behind me in high school, but I noticed how kind and sweet you were. You had a friend at school with a leg brace, and I admired that you'd waited patiently to walk with her to the next room. Have I really put my foot in my mouth?"

"I can't say that I don't remember you. You have a younger brother too. Isn't that right? I knew you were on the football team and it seemed there was always a cheerleader hanging off your arm."

The symbolism of the cheerleader jerked her memory to the afternoon when Bethany was testing her wiles.

"I protest," Jackson teased. "You have the wrong impression of me then. I'll admit I dated a few girls from school but never anything serious. I actually considered inviting you as my prom date but couldn't get up the courage. Yes, my brother is Jarvis, but regrettably, I don't see him much."

"I'm flattered, and I guess we're both guilty of noticing each other. I'm sorry you don't get to spend time with Jarvis."

Deep in thought, he reached for her hand.

"Speaking of cheerleaders," she said, "I saw you earlier today, with Bethany hanging off your arm. I was hauling toy trains to my car when I saw her snuggling up to you."

"Hey, Pol, don't even think it. I told her point blank that I'm interested in someone else. That's the truth. I've been smitten."

"Then I owe you an apology, Jackson, I guess I found myself experiencing a bit of jealousy, which I'm not used to dealing with."

"I adore your innocent truths and I'm relieved."

"Relieved?"

Jackson smirked and nodded.

As the brass section of the town band started up, the lights began to flicker in syncopation across the park, illuminating hundreds of pines and bushes, finally reaching the massive decorated Christmas tree.

The crowd cheered and roared as the night was transformed into an illuminated fantasyland, with children laughing and dancing in the snow between the ice sculptures, still wound up from the morning Santa Claus parade.

"I love all of this," she said. "In fact, everything about the season. Does your family gather on Christmas Day?"

Jackson looked away she noticed a hesitancy. "I took Wayne's Christmas schedule so he could be with his family. My parents and my brother are spending a few days at the Chateau Montebello to ski. And you?"

"Last year was the exception and we didn't celebrate," she said. But I'm determined to make this the best one ever for Tim and Kate. We'll have a family-run feast at our house on Christmas Day for folks who don't have family nearby."

"That's incredible! Kind of a Christmas dinner for the homeless," he joked.

"So far, it's just me, Tim and Kate, and Kate's friend and her grandmother." Her eyes danced with excitement. "You're welcome to come if you'd like. There will be lots to eat and I confess that I'm a good cook."

"Although I'll work on Christmas Day, I get a dinner break. Could I join you for a short while? I'd like to have Christmas with you."

With a flutter in her heart, she wished she could instantly twirl around a room with her handsome prince, but common sense returned.

"I'd really like that. We'll plan dinner around your schedule."

As he squeezed her hand, a warm feeling came over him, as if he were going home for Christmas.

Jackson's personable nature shielded the outside world from his real heartache and loneliness. He'd been on his own since college, and at twenty-seven, he was proud of the changes and decisions in his life, becoming defiant in the rights of justice to protect underprivileged and challenged folks.

With odd jobs, he put himself through Police Academy and moved back to his roots in Lac Maurice four years ago, but couldn't bear to return to Hanson Ridge, with its too many unpleasant memories.

When not working weekends, he visited nearby towns to serve at homeless shelters, hoping to someday see the face of his younger brother, Jarvis, who had stormed out of the house years before after a confrontation with his drunken father. Jarvis had tired of the nightly rows with father and watching the agony on the face of his mother.

Growing up was fraught with ups and downs. In spite of his father's alcoholism and his mother's infidelities, the family remained a unit living at Grandfather Tripp's house on Hanson Ridge.

Now he didn't know where they were, his brother or either parent. It was easier to say they were skiing at Chateau Montebello than explain to Polly about the family fracture.

Jackson was six-foot and muscular. His jet black hair was always immaculately groomed, trimmed at the local barbershop every second Monday. Frequently, folks mentioned the unique color in his eyes. He stood out as a handsome, eligible bachelor in the community, and past attempts at matchmaking made him uncomfortable. Despite others' good intentions, he tended to be a loner rather than endure having single women shoved his way.

The band struck up *I'll be Home for Christmas*, and as Polly gripped his arm, he glanced at the loose golden curls that escaped her hat.

I'm not looking for a date or a nightlife, but a solid home based on love. I'd almost given up hope that I might find a girl in Lac Maurice until Polly Perkins caught my eye and here she is at my side. Polly's responsibility for two siblings doesn't scare me. I wish I had done more for Jarvis, but perhaps I can now be a positive influence for Kate and Tim.

Polly had no idea the future was being considered by this man at her side, but it was the first time since the fateful day a year ago that she felt at ease. The devastation had been unimaginable, and she knew Kate and Tim were going through the same, all fearful of what might happen yet desperate to cling together.

Tim, seventeen, was now keeping too much to himself, almost defiant and even devious about his whereabouts. Polly craved for advice to guide him and prayed for wisdom. Kate, on the other hand, seemed more like her daughter than her sister and she relied on their chats.

Polly's head was jammed with colliding emotions.

I can't expect Jackson to step into my life and fix everything. It wouldn't be fair to him or to Tim and Kate. I just hope for good judgment as I have the spontaneous passion of my great-grandmother and my grandmother. From what I've read of the diaries it's clear to me that we Winslow and Perkins women rule our lives with our hearts.

Business was brisk at the hot chocolate hut near the roaring bonfire, manned by Peggy's staff in elves' hats. A brass quartet created a rhythm for swaying and dancing and a crowd of townsfolk lined into a spontaneous circle around the band shell, singing lively carols. At ease now, Polly tilted her head with a childlike plea. "Feel like caroling?"

As he led her into the crowd, she leaned her head against his coat. "I haven't even tried to sing since I was a boy. But I'll fake and fumble through this one."

The chorus of voices filled the park:

'Joy to the World, the Lord is come;
Let earth receive her King,
Let every heart prepare him room
And Heaven and nature sing.'

In the throng, she imagined her father's deep bass. Closing her eyes, she picked out the soprano warble of Maddie Perkins, in her memory, hitting the highest notes when everyone else strained. Instead, it was Wendy Beaton from the Baptist Church choir who hit the shrill ones.

"Hear her piercing warble?" she teased. "Listen for it, Jackson, and you'll hear it again in the next one."

"You're a special woman, Polly Perkins."

In the glow of colored lights, she saw Kate and Monica across the park, and on tiptoes, she looked for any sign of Tim.

Precisely at seven, the marching parade began from the town hall parking lot, where Carson Fergus had lined up the float wagons pulled by old trucks or teams of Clydesdales with flowing hooves and manes. Mr. Heard and his son proudly corralled a cluster of sheep from the nativity while Rolly, the Collie, circled to keep them in order. Mary, Joseph, and the baby were towed in a tiny hay cart.

The hardware store sponsored Santa's float, led by the 4-H Club's string of decorated ponies wearing reindeer ears.

Out in front were the oompahs of the town band marching in step down Sugarbush.

Representing the peasants who fought in the Rebellion of 1837, Emery Butler wore a patriot uniform, walking beside his wife in a pilgrim dress and bonnet. In front was a lad carrying a sign for Butler's Steakhouse.

Behind the peasants, Hank Moffatt pounded the beat on a snare drum strapped to his shoulder. Ezra Stockton, the owner of the Hardware store and his clerk, Dan, marched in a group of out-of-tune trumpets marching out of step.

A few of Kate's friends waved to her from the baton troop, bundled in leotards and short skirts, twirling batons in one hand and juggling pompoms in the other.

Once the contingent arrived at the park, town councilor Berman gave his greetings and promoted the Christmas trees at the church lot where Santa would have his reindeer and sleigh.

"Profits on the tree sales will go to the food bank. Please bring canned foods or a donation to Rev. Dennison to help the less fortunate and the homeless, so no one in Lac Maurice goes hungry this Christmas."

Polly whispered, "We'll bring some canned food from home."

She heard herself use the word 'we' for the first time, and was pleased with how it sounded.

"I haven't had a tree in years," he said. "Have you got one yet?"

Jackson was distracted by the mention of the homeless at Christmas and he wondered about his missing brother.

Polly shook her head. "This is the perfect night to get one, but Kate always helps . . . wait for us at the tree lot." In an instant, she was back with Kate and Monica.

"Spruce or pine, Kate?"

"That's tough. Dad preferred spruce but Mom loved the smell of pine."

"Then pine it must be."

Kate went straight to the tallest ones.

"Jackson, with your height, can you pick out a beauty for us, like that one? But Pol, I'm going for hot chocolate with my friends and I'll see you at home."

From the thick of the lot, he dragged back a seven-foot jack pine.

"How's this? Too tall?"

"The ceiling should be high enough, or we'll take a speck off the trunk."

"I'll have it strapped to my truck and bring it right away. Are you ready, Pol?"

She smiled that he used her shortened name, used affectionately by Tim and Kate, Peg and Sophia.

I'm glad he's comfortable with that.

Through the wet flakes melting on her windshield, she marveled at the colored lights forming the shape of her house in the distance. In her eyes tonight, her century home resembled a magical castle with the lights sparkling across the snow.

Jackson pulled into the lane behind her. He sprung the pine from its tethers and dragged it to the huge veranda, leaning it against one of the stately pillars.

"This grand house reminds me of when my grandparents lived at Hanson Ridge. I loved Christmases there." He gripped the frozen tree. "Where do we put Jack?"

"It's always in the living room window. We can set it up and let the branches relax overnight. Tomorrow, after church, Kate, Tim and I will decorate. Are you able to join us?"

Jackson tried to be diplomatic with his reply. "You're trying to juggle a family here . . . as much as I'd like it, I should give you some space."

His gesture was gallant and well-intended but didn't convince Polly.

"My grandmother would say, Pshaw!"

"What was that she said? Say it again."

"Pshaw, pshaw. It's up to you, Jackson. You are welcome and I hope you accept the offer."

After he left, she waited by the fireplace. At about ten, footsteps at the door woke her and Kate burst in carrying a faint whiff of cigarette smoke. Polly wrinkled her nose.

"Kate, are you alright?"

"Thanks for waiting up, Pol, but I don't want to talk now. I'm going to my room—I have a nasty headache."

With Tim still out, Polly curled up again, then opened her eyes wide toward the Winslow box. She picked out a pink adolescent diary with a broken clasp.

It was from 1954 when Maddie was ten. A handwritten inscription was in the front: "Dear Maddie with all my love, a diary can be your dearest friend in all the world."

This time Polly imagined her grandmother as a girl, reading and writing in this beloved journal.

> November 20, 1954. Dear diary, I got you for my Birthday and I'd like us to be friends. It was so groovy at the school dance and I learned the Jitterbug. Oh, what fun it was, although some say it's not wholesome to dance fast like that. The Christmas dance is scheduled for the last day of school before the holiday break. I'm dreaming that Roger Hanson asks me to dance.

"Not another mention of Hanson," Polly said aloud. "It can't be . . ." She put it back and opened a later diary, jumping ahead three years.

"June 6, 1957. Graduation is in two weeks. All the girls are having fancy dresses made but Mom insists that I go to Montreal with her and buy something far out with glam and glitter. I've applied to Amnesty International for a summer internship in London or anywhere as long as I get away from Lac Maurice. I need to get away from prying eyes. I've given up on Roger Hanson."

Polly accepted the last entry as good news, then stopped to ponder Tim's situation and behavior.

"I wonder if he desperately wants out of Lac Maurice to get a fresh start and not be haunted by ghosts every day."

When the grandfather clock struck midnight, she put the box away, but as she laid it down, something jingled inside.

In a corner, she found a tiny, heart-shaped golden locket on a broken neck chain, with etched initials A.W. and W.H. The hinge was stiff and she couldn't open the facing, which she imagined had a picture of long-lost lovers.

It was Polly's character to resolve problems, but with the late hour and no immediate clues in her mind, she went up to bed with her thoughts troubled.

She drifted off watched the ceiling as she listened for Tim on the stairs or the hall. At 2:30 she was awakened and felt sickened.

"Why did he need Grandfather's pocket watch? He could have come and talked if he had a problem."

Jackson's words echoed back to her.

"Sometimes a boy just needs another man to talk to."

8

She was the only one stirring in the morning after a restless night. A sound sleep was impossible as her imagination ran in so many directions.

"What terrible things could be taking place in Tim's life?"

Sitting up on her bed, Polly stared at the wallpaper, remembering her Mother letting her choose this pattern of twisted lavender roses and ivy trails. It seemed so long ago and carried so many memories.

"I've looked at this wallpaper during times of joy and sadness. It's time to redecorate as an adult. Perhaps even to move into the master bedroom. Coffee! That's what I need to sort my thoughts with a clear head."

At seven o'clock, she listened to a tap at the front door and covered up in a housecoat. She peered through the curtain, and attempting a futile adjustment to her hair, she opened the door.

"Jackson. What's the matter? You look troubled."

"Can I come in for coffee?" he whispered. "I don't want to wake up Kate or Tim."

"Of course. We'll talk in the dining room. The sounds won't carry upstairs. Get settled and I'll be back. Two creams, one sugar, right?"

"I probably shouldn't be here, but I know how hard you try to look after your brother and sister."

"Your tone is scaring me, Jackson. Out with it, please. Does it have something to do with Tim?"

"Afraid so."

"He didn't get home last night until two-thirty. I've been sick wondering what's going on."

"It's not that bad . . . but he was present with a group of teenagers when a night raid was made on a known drug house outside of town. The police determined he wasn't involved, but he was there as a bystander."

He paused to give Polly a chance to absorb it.

"However, if he is ever found with drugs or affiliating with that gang, they won't turn a blind eye next time."

"Why isn't he in jail right now?"

"When I got home last night, Wayne was arriving and told me about the raid. If Wayne hadn't helped, Tim would be in jail. It scared the living daylights out of Tim."

Polly's hand trembled as she put down her cup.

"I don't know what I'm supposed to do. I am his legal guardian for another year. At eighteen he gets his college trust fund and can do as he pleases."

"I went to the station right away and waited with Tim until the bondsman came. He was shaken up and could barely speak. I posted his bail and brought him home."

"Did he talk to you about it?"

"He was tight-lipped at first but eventually I earned his confidence."

"What happens now?"

"I told him to get a good sleep and that I'd come this afternoon for the tree decorating. He feels ashamed to face you and asked me to help him."

"I can't thank you enough, Jackson. I planned to skip church this morning, but it's likely best if I'm out of the house when Tim comes down. He needs to feel secure in his own home."

"See, you have all the parental instincts you need. I'm bushed and I'll go home for some shut-eye and a shower. If it's alright, Polly, I'll bring pizza and we'll meet here at noon."

Polly placed her hand on Jackson's. "I can't tell you how grateful I am . . . for being my friend, my confidant, and my gala date."

"Gala date? That doesn't sound romantic at all." She stretched on her toes for a forehead kiss.

"Your Mom would enjoy this fresh pine aroma. This place is looking a lot like Christmas."

In her regular church pew, Polly expected critical eyes upon her with the supposition that everyone in town knew of Tim's detainment. She was certain the catty ones would conjecture that poor Tim, without a real mother, was bound to falter.

She was glad for the distraction of Rev. Dennison's words from the book of Luke: "They brought two turtle doves signifying faithfulness and eternal love."

She romanticized in her thoughts.

When I was a little girl, Mother used to read me The Twelve Days of Christmas. It seemed so Victorian, but my favorite line had the two turtle doves . . . it was romantic even then. Perhaps if I make it through the twelve days of Christmas, Jackson will be my turtle dove."

She closed her eyes with a broad smile.

The foyer hummed with chatter as she made her way to the door. Whispers abounded in her imagination, and she turned to look directly in the eyes of two gossiping women.

"That's poor Tim's mother . . . the younger ones should have been sent away . . . Polly's doing her best."

At the door, Rev. Dennison used his most sympathetic tone. "How are you doing, Polly?"

"I'm well, thank you. This time of year has difficult memories for my family, but it is a time when I know who my true friends are. Christmas is a time when the community comes together to support those less fortunate . . . with words of compassion and not judgment." Polly's words carried the right amount of acrimony.

"Bless you, dear child."

She passed Jackson's truck outside the pizza parlor and knew that seeing him at the house would boost her spirits.

Arriving home, the stereo was turned up high, and from the door, she could hear laughter as the voices of Tim and Kate bantered about the Christmas decorations he brought up from storage. "Hey, Tim. Jackson is bringing pizza for lunch and will stay for decorating."

Just then, Kate raced past to the upper level. A minute later, she rode down the great mahogany banister, something her mother had forbidden. But she knew she'd get away with such mischief with Polly.

"See, Pol, I did the dusting," Kate beamed and rubbed a shine with her sleeve onto the end post.

"Every little bit helps, Kate," Polly said, biting her tongue.

They all stopped at the sound of Jackson's tires crunching into the driveway.

"He's here," Tim said.

"Decorating is on hold!" Polly shouted. "It's the pizza guy."

In the kitchen, he greeted her with a long kiss.

"Your aftershave," she whispered and kissed him again. "It's delightful."

He slid into the empty kitchen chair beside Polly, her mother's favorite and rarely used by the others.

A bridge of hot cheese dangled from Tim's mouth and he covered it with his hand before Kate would poke fun at it.

"Thanks for the pizza," he said. "It's nice to have another man in the house. You can't imagine the agony I go through living with two girls."

Tim looked at the others expecting laughter.

"You should have said you were bothered," Polly said. "I hope you're kidding."

"You do just fine eating our cooking," Kate added, "not to mention our housekeeping."

"Timeout." "Jackson raised his hand. "I say enjoy each other while you can. You never know when life turns a corner."

"It was a poor joke," Tim said. "I didn't mean to hurt any feelings."

"Tim, I had an idea, when you told me about an assignment on politics and law. Would you like to join me and Wayne on some ride-alongs? It'll give you a look at what we do and how the town is run."

"Would I? That would be awesome!"

"I'll warn you we drink a lot of coffee and eat fast food."

"And donuts?" Polly teased. She eased back in her chair as she silently watched a magical transformation of Tim. She slid her hand onto Jackson's knee.

Kate turned a radio station to *Rockin' around the Christmas Tree* and sat down again, wiggling and snapping at her chair until finally giving in and jumping up to dance, with her limbs twirling badly in all directions.

Rockin' around the Christmas tree,
At the Christmas party hop.
Mistletoe hung where you can see,
Every couple tries to stop…
Rockin' around the Christmas tree
Let the Christmas spirit ring
Later we'll have some pumpkin pie
And we'll do some caroling…

"Come on, guys," Kate said, clapping as she swayed. "Show your Christmas spirit. Jackson, can you hang the mistletoe over the arch? You're the tallest one."

Polly rooted in the box and handed out the ornaments for the tree.

"Remember when we were tiny and all the ornaments would be on the lowest branch?" Kate said. "I love those memories."

"The lights get strung first," Tim said, "then these big golden balls."

"I like these little ceramic people, like this wee lady ornament with the teensy violin." Every item from the box was passed around drawing precious recollections.

With the angel planted at the top, everyone joined in the customary 'oohs and aahs'.

At the fireplace mantle, Polly lifted the photo of her parents on their twenty-fifth anniversary, then her eyes went to the Winslow box on the floor.

"See, Mom, this will be a good Christmas after all. Look at Tim and Kate smiling, and I know you would approve of my wonderful Jackson. Great-grandmother Winslow would be pleased I found her diaries too."

Jackson put his hands on her shoulders from behind. "Is it like you remember, Polly?"

"Exactly!"

"What about you? Did you have family tree-decorating afternoons like this?"

"I'd rather enjoy this moment than bring back my old memories. Right here and now—this is the way Christmas should always be."

Tim blurted out, "Polly, I won't mind if Jackson comes for Christmas dinner."

"Now don't get soft," Jackson laughed. "I'll manage a break to be here, I promise."

"Have you invited anyone, Tim?" Polly asked from the kitchen.

"Not yet" His face was grim. "I'm good with lots of guests but I also liked our old family dinners where we could just be ourselves."

Just as Polly burst in with a tray of mugs, Jackson announced, "I'm sorry, everyone. I need to go as I'm on the night shift today."

"Not so fast!" Polly said. "My hot chocolate first. It's tradition after the tree."

Jackson sagged back into Seymour's over-stuffed armchair and she cozied up on the arm.

On the TV in the background, crowds gathered at the lighting of the tree at Rockefeller Centre. Tim turned up the volume for the music, as the headliners were right up his alley, the likes of Pearl Jam, Aerosmith and Lenny Kravitz.

"Awesome!" Tim said. "Think we could drive to New York sometime, Polly?"

She nodded. "If it's something we all want."

Jackson added, "Everyone should travel, but Christmas is a time to be at home with family."

He took a sprig of mistletoe from the side table and attached it over the entry. "Thank you for today, Kate . . . and Perkins family."

Kate lingered after for a sisters' chat. "You've got your heart set on him, don't you?"

"We don't have control over what our hearts choose. You're fourteen now—surely there's a boy or two that makes your heart beat a step faster. I'm learning that our line of women has thrived on passion."

"That's good, isn't it?"

"Yes, that's good."

"There is a boy from Hanson Ridge. He's new to Lac Maurice. I seem to gravitate to people that need a friend or a little support."

"Mother would be proud to hear you say that. She taught and showed us how to be kind-hearted and considerate of others. That's a reason for our Christmas feast this year to include others less fortunate."

"Less fortunate than you and Timmy and me," Kate said. "We have each other."

9

His evening shifts conflicted with any chance of romance in the following week and Polly couldn't even manage to cross paths with him at Sal's on her way to work. She hoped even for the sight of him in his uniform, but the closest she got was seeing his tail lights turn a corner up ahead.

In recent days, Jackson had found a new motivation within himself to seek out Jarvis. Beyond his normal Wednesday night serving supper at area homeless shelters, he took any available evening and his scant spare hours to continue his search.

On Monday, he picked Tim up from school to begin their ride-along. Polly waited up late to see Tim's reaction and with hopes of a glimpse of the man that had stolen her heart.

As a distraction and with her mind carrying the legal threat on the property, she returned to the document box and the locket.

With a thin dime, she picked away at the heart's opening, finally giving way and popping open.

A miniature photo of a young couple made her heart pound. "Who are they and why is it in my treasure box?"

The woman was striking, with a high bouffant and wispy curls, and eyes that seemed sparkling and deep, even in black and white and the gentleman was meticulous with a pencil-thin dark mustache.

The grandfather clock in the foyer struck eleven as Tim turned the key. , looking up at her immediately with a look of contentment that Polly hadn't seen in a long time.

"You didn't need to wait up."

"I have a deal. I'll make you a sandwich as you tell me all the details."

"You wouldn't believe what fun we had!"

Polly sat out a plate of tuna salad sandwiches with two big glasses of cold milk.

"There was a lady in the country, Mrs. Ferguson. Her husband is a truck driver and was away when she went into labor. There wasn't time to call the medics so Officer Wayne delivered the baby. Mrs. Ferguson said she didn't mind if I wanted to watch a miracle happen. The tiniest little fingers and toes and the thrill of his first cry. It truly was a miracle, incredible seeing the beginning of a new life."

He paused to sort out an idea. "Polly, do you think I could get a little gift for Mrs. Ferguson's baby? The baby seems extra special to me."

"It's wonderful that you got to see that. Most folks go through life and never see God's handy work in the creation of a baby. I have cash in my wallet. Take what you need."

"Thanks." He took a couple bites. "There's a night bar in the seedy part of town that I never knew existed. They called about a raucous in the alley. When we got there, both Wayne and Jackson turned tough and straightened those guys out. It was part of a bully gang with switchblades.

"In the alley, crumpled beside empty cardboard boxes, Jackson noticed a man who had been badly beaten and kicked. He spoke to him kindly and helped him back onto his feet, then we took him to the jail so he could have a warm bed and a hot meal."

"Wow! Such a contrast in the incidents," Polly said. "It must be hard for an officer to determine on the spot between compassion and hard discipline."

"We waited in the car for more calls, but it was quiet so we talked, drank coffee and nibbled on donuts. Coming home on the town road, we saw a car in the ditch with its headlights on, and they found an elderly man slumped in the driver's seat. Wayne and Jackson helped him out and called an ambulance, and Jackson performed CPR. I asked Jackson if there's a place I can take first aid. It was awesome, Mom!"

Polly was very touched. She noticed the slip of his tongue but showed no reaction to avoid embarrassment.

"That's quite a night. Aren't you tired?"

"I'm exhausted," he laughed. "But I need to slow down my adrenaline. You go to bed and I'll see you in the morning. I'll watch TV before I go up."

Tim's kindness warmed her heart. "A page has turned for Tim, I believe."

On Thursday morning, with two more days to the Policeman's Ball, Polly hadn't heard from Jackson, between his soup kitchen drives and overtime shifts.

Needing a boost, she stopped at Sal's for morning coffee.

"Mornin' Polly. Jackson was by here yesterday was talking about the Policeman's Ball. Said he's going with the most beautiful girl in all of Lac Maurice . . . his words."

"I'm relieved. The weekend was perfect but I haven't heard too much from him since. He sure has been busy, but he knows how to reach me."

"Don't fret. You're so lucky going to the Ball. It's talked about year round and most of the officers are married. Girls would line up for a handsome bachelor like yours. You've hooked yourself a real prize."

"I don't need to be reminded of that!"

"Is your coffee to stay or are you running late, Polly?"

"To go. Sophia will be in this morning for a chat, so double it in fact."

She scurried along to the store, irked again that the town could be so nosy.

"Would line up for a bachelor! Hmmf!"

"My display window will be whimsical when the new train display is lit up and whirling across the countryside. I hope people will come."

At a shop workbench, she painted the names of local businesses on the facades of her miniature buildings. With tweezers, she adjusted the greenery and the tiniest of lights, then poured the steam liquid into the engines and checked the batteries and transformers.

The miniature courtyard and town hall were set in the center with a tall maypole, with tiny white lights draped from the pole's tip and anchored to the wall, creating a ceiling of stars.

She stepped out to the street to admire the train and her strategic placements of antique dolls, lanterns, brass bells, rocking chairs, and Coca-Cola Santa stand-ups.

Splendid at last with imitation snow, it was a little girl's fantasy. As the train whirred and tooted, its lights shone over the dolls. The chugging, puffing, and whirring sounds were climaxed by the toot-toot of the engine as it rounded the corner of the display.

"Ah, Sophia is here, through the back!"

The radio was playing *Baby, It's Cold Outside* and Sophia was aggressively humming in time with Bette Midler, interjecting words she knew and making up those she didn't.

"Good morning, Sunshine!" Polly called over the music.

"Polly, isn't it a wonderful time of year?"

Sophia wore a light Santa hat with a tassel, and a red felt apron with bells and balls embroidered across the bodice and along the hem.

"I forgot, today's the day we agreed to start wearing our festive costumes."

"I brought an extra that's hanging in the back room."

"Did you talk with Edith about our evening out?" Polly asked as she tied on an apron.

"We know you have a few galas on the horizon, but would Wednesday work? We like Colonel Butler's for a nice ambiance. Everyone feels special there."

"Perfect, I'll arrange it. Since you are Santa's Elf, I have an accessory you should have now. It's a token of how much you mean to me, not only as my co-worker but as my friend and substitute mother."

From her handbag, she took a small box in shimmering gold and a red curly ribbon.

"Ah, I just give motherly advice as the urge comes."

The two laughed, as Sophia tore at the wrap. Inside was a pearl and oyster shell poinsettia pin set on a porcelain green wreath and encrusted with tiny diamonds.

"Ah, 'tis beautiful to feast me eyes on," Sophia squealed.

"I didn't know that you were Irish, Soph."

"I'm not. It was on a movie last night, one of those lines that can stick with you. I've been waiting to try it out."

Bustling about the store, the two chatted nonsense until Sophia froze with her hand in the air.

"Oh, Polly, I forgot to tell you, Mrs. Warner called as I arrived. She wants the other candelabra too. Withers will come by around noon to collect it."

"I can't say I'm surprised. I always say more is better than less. She's of the same mind it seems."

While packing it, Polly thought about the missing pocket watch.

"Sophia, is there a pawn shop in town where someone could get cash for say . . . a watch?"

"From time to time, we get someone down on their luck trying to sell us antiques. Otherwise, I can't think of any place. You'd have to go to out of town for that."

"Have we had a gold pocket watch here in the last while?"

"Are you thinking of one for Jackson for Christmas?"

"Oh no, we're not serious like that, but I suppose I should consider getting him something. He's agreed to come for Christmas dinner." She knew she'd confessed a fib—they were indeed serious.

"I know it sounds mundane, but VanDorn's Men Store had woolen scarves in their window. That's always safe."

"What if I want to do more than be safe, what's next?"

"Something sentimental of an event or discussion that you've shared. Maybe a photo of the two of you."

"That sounds presumptuous. I'll see how our date goes on Saturday. We'll drive to Quebec City and it's so scenic, even at night."

Friday night, Polly was on pins and needles, imagining Jackson as her Prince and she was the Princess with the glass slipper.

"I want to capture the moment in my memory . . . the look in his eyes when he sees me on the staircase."

After breakfast, she again went through her mother's sentimental jewelry and closet of elegant gowns and cocktail dresses.

"Mother was the belle of the ball in her day, always regal—the way Mrs. Warner stands, tall and erect. Even as grey seeped into her hair, it just looked better and the blonde highlights prevented signs of aging."

Polly sat down at her mother's dressing table. "I'll wear my hair up with these drop diamond earrings and the ruby pendant with the crest of wee diamond chips. Yes . . ." She held her hair up with one hand and dangled the earring with the other. "Yes, I have a long enough neck."

Kate snuck up behind Polly as she preened in front of the dressing mirror.

"You'll knock 'em dead, Pol. All you need now are Mother's diamond pins to hold your hair in place. Let's see." Kate fumbled into the jewelry box until she found four.

"Fabulous idea, Kate! Are you home tonight to help me get ready?"

Kate hesitated. "I was going to go to a movie with friends, but if this is important to you, I'll be here."

"Oh, no, Kate, I'll be fine on my own. Go ahead with your plans."

10

With Saturday afternoon to herself, Polly organized her files across the library table to check in with Myrna Sutcliffe, hoping to find more about Harris Winslow and his claim against the Perkins family.

"No reason to alarm Kate and Tim about the situation. It seems to have been family disagreement, that he severed his family relationship, perhaps jealousy and resentment. I can resolve it on my own. Father dealt with Mr. Silvester at the law firm next to the Commerce Bank. I'll take him what I've found on Monday."

An afterthought struck her and she returned to the shop to collect the clump of papers taken from her father's roll top. Then she continued on to the library.

On a notebook, she wrote out pages for the lawyer, including relevant names of voters that had lived on Cricklecreek Road: Franklin Winslow, Millicent Winslow,

Madeleine Winslow, and Stanley Harris Winslow and his wife Margery.

Harris Jr. was sent away to McGill University and rarely attended family gatherings. While he was away, Stanley Harris and Margery were victims of an airplane crash in the Caribbean, leaving their only son with no other immediate family.

In the McGill mid-80s Alumni, she found that Harris Jr. had graduated and went to work at a Montreal accounting firm. Speculating in penny stocks, he blew the remains of his inheritance and his parents' life insurance in a few years. More digging turned up a Montreal newspaper item of a DUI charge and a subsequent lawsuit.

The sad truth of Cousin Harris Winslow is in black and white. It seems he was something of a jet-setter in his prime. He was lobbying for funding to start up a technology firm and was looking for backers, but it generated lawsuits suggesting fraud. It appears he became desperate to keep his head above water."

Transfixed in sorting out the family puzzle, Polly set her mind to go head-on with Harris to clear the air and find a solution.

"I'll talk to Jackson first, but if Tim and Kate agree, perhaps the kindest position would be to invite Cousin Harris to our Christmas dinner. Am I even being realistic? He's obviously down and out on his luck and may have nowhere to turn."

Near the outskirts of town, an idea struck her, and with a U-turn, she pulled up in front of Laurier Antiques.

"Bonjour, Monsieur Laurier."

"My goodness, my old friend, Polly. I'm sorry I haven't seen you since the funeral. I hope all is well."

"Thank you for your kind words. Could you help me? I'm wondering if anyone came here last week offering to sell you a gold pocket watch."

"Gold pocket watch?" Mr. Laurier scratched his chin and led her to a locked, glass-top jewelry case.

"This is what we have."

Polly's eyes immediately went to it. "How much for that one? I need it as a gift."

"The young man that sold it asked me to hold it a few weeks until he could buy it back. I'm not in the business of a pawnbroker, but he seemed sincere and desperate."

"May I have a look at it?"

The storekeeper pulled out a velvet tray where Polly could inspect it under the light. She smiled at the inscription. "How much do you need, Mr. Laurier?"

"I believe I gave the lad a hundred dollars. It's worth far more. I did give him my promise…"

"Yes, I can see that it is. I'll give you back your one hundred dollars and another fifty for your trouble. You see, this is a family heirloom that went astray. Once it is back where it belongs, I assure you that your promise will be upheld."

"Goodness gracious, you mean it was stolen?"

"Now that I have it back, we'll just say it was borrowed."

Monsieur Laurier was trembling, fearing that he had been involved in some way.

"Please, Sir, do me a great honor of keeping this between us." She leaned in waiting for him to relax and smile.

"Indeed, Polly. You and your family have a Merry Christmas."

"We certainly will and thank you so very much. My father always said you were a good and fair man."

When she pulled into her driveway, it was almost four o'clock. Jackson would be picking her up in an hour and the drive to Quebec City wouldn't take more than an hour and a half.

"For a supposedly quiet Saturday, I'd say I've been pretty busy. I still have time for a bubble bath with some calming lavender candles. It seems no one else is home."

She tucked the watch in the secret box on her closet shelf. It felt good to have the soft silk robe against her skin as she tiptoed to fill the claw tub in the master suite.

"Ah, wonderful. Nothing like Epsom salts to relax . . . and to think."

She sat upright and minutes later went to the phone. Her mind should have been on an elegant evening ahead, but instead, she dialed Milton Marlborough's office.

The conversation was lengthy and she related the findings from her documents, of the history of Harris Jr., of the trust fund in lieu of property that he'd received and squandered, with examples of character deficiencies of fraud and deceit that had led to his personal misfortune.

By three forty-five, the anticipation had built her spirits to a high, and she laughed at herself when the doorbell rang.

"Oops, there's nobody home to let Jackson in. I was planning on an elegant entrance down the staircase."

The sight of him took her breath away, freshly shaven, in a formal, silk, black tuxedo, and a white scarf. She held the door open to cherish the moment, feeling his gaze peering into her soul. The tingling in her toes started again.

His hand extended a corsage box with a wrist floral of white roses entwined with silver leaves and ivy. The thoughtful florist advised that the white rose would be a gentle flower indicating young love.

Carefully, he slid it onto Polly's wrist as if he had spent time practicing.

"You look magnificent," he said.

"Funny, that's what I was thinking about you. The corsage is beautiful. Thank you, Jackson, I'm so ready for this evening."

"Everyone at the ball will be envious. Polly, I can't tell you what this means, having you on my arm."

She let herself fall into the brown eyes with sparkles of emeralds.

"It's like you're my turtle dove, Jackson."

"You don't expect me to know what that means, but I do. Two turtle doves . . . yes, I like that."

Polly's black, slinky dress hugged her figure, with a slit in the skirt rising above her knee. Her porcelain neck was draped with diamonds with a few wisps and half-twisted strands of golden hair.

She handed him her mother's black brocade cape with fur trim and he wrapped her like an envelope, then leaned his face against hers with a soft kiss.

"A carriage awaits my lady," he said.

The limousine passed through the St. Louis Gates on Quebec City's Rue des Carriers, down a tree-lined cobbled street past the Plains of Abraham. A parade of black limos from towns across the province took turns in the queue at the arched portico of the Chateau Frontenac.

The hotel, a magnificent castle, overlooked the St. Lawrence and the lower town, the site of the habitation built by Champlain four hundred years before.

Inside was a magical winter theme with white and silver frosted trees. The marble floors and plush carpets were accented by a hand-woven tapestry and gold epaulets over the grand floor-to-ceiling windows, and the ceilings were encased with seventeenth-century paintings.

In a dignified monotone, a maître d' announced his name from a parchment scroll. "Sergeant Jackson Tripp et Mademoiselle Pollyanna Perkins."

Instantly, a champagne tray appeared and a tuxedoed waiter walked in front to the ballroom, passing a group of carolers in vintage costumes. A few feet inside, a line of French waitresses met them with platters of hors-d'oeuvres and delicacies.

Every nook or cranny was festive with lavish Christmas trees and wreaths and giant gold balls and ribbons suspended from the high ceiling. A group of uniformed officers dignified with polished brass awards was being piped in to be seated at a head table.

"Oh, Jackson, it's like a Cinderella ball. Surely we are among royalty and aristocrats."

Polly surveyed the room for a familiar face, as Wayne and Cynthia spied them from across the ballroom. "Wow! Polly, your dress is gorgeous!"

"Cynthia, you are so kind . . . thank you. Yours is breathtaking; the red sequins and flared skirt are exquisite."

Wayne insisted that she twirl a pirouette to show it off.

"We shopped in Montreal for it," Cynthia said. "A romantic weekend and we took in some theatre."

"It was my duty," Wayne started. "It cost me an arm and a leg . . ."

Jackson poked him and winked. As partners, they knew each another like brothers and he knew to prevent Wayne from starting up his marriage jokes. Wayne's booming voice could captivate a crowd easily enough.

"Excuse us," he said. "I'll make some introductions for Polly. I see our Captain from Charlesbourg."

Guiding her across the room, she was enthralled with the hotel's European influence.

"This is a castle," she said, "and a dream."

11

With the sweet background strains of violins and cellos, teams of white-jacketed servers circled the tables with five gourmet courses and wine pairings. As the performance awards wound up during dessert, the audience rose with applause to honor those that lost loved ones in service.

As lights dimmed, the ceiling sparkled as if under an umbrella of what seemed to be a thousand stars. A dance orchestra came to life on the stage, and the police captains led the first waltz.

It never occurred to me that I'd ever waltz, but I'll follow Jackson. It can't be that hard.

Jackson reached for her hand. "Mademoiselle Pollyanna Perkins, may I have your first dance?"

Resisting the urge to giggle, she raised her wrist to him and melted into his eyes, then stood to be swept away.

"Yes, Jackson. We're two turtle doves. But I warn you I haven't danced in years."

A Viennese Waltz had started and they blended into the center. Floating with the music, Polly felt the magic and harmony of being so close to her man, starting a new and unexpected chapter in her life.

His face brushed hers, and he pulled her closer until she felt his heart.

"Pol, I've never been to these balls before. I didn't know anyone until now that I would want to spend such an evening with."

She whispered, "Thanks, Jackson. I'm glad I was the only one. I don't want this to ever end."

Nothing else needed to be said.

The evening flew by and the pulse turned to an old-fashioned minuet, then a folk dance, jive, salsa, and the music of the 70's and 80's.

Too soon for them, the band stopped and a spotlight shone on the midnight buffet. "It's a precursor to closing the bar, Polly. Can I get you anything before we call our limo?"

"It's been wonderful, but I'll have to agree with my feet— they are insisting on their displeasure with these new shoes."

"Rest them here. I'll get your cape and call the driver."

Polly watched every step he took to the door. "I wish mother could see what a fine man you are, Jackson."

As she waited, Cynthia Crawford joined her. "You two looked very cozy. Jackson is a real gem, Polly"

"Those are the words exactly. I know little about his past, but he has swept me off my feet."

"Sometimes you shouldn't dig up old wounds."

"What do you mean?

"Jackson hasn't always had a happy life. He's had a painful past. He rarely talks about it, but I see that you are bringing him out of his shell."

Curiosity would nudge and bait her for the rest of the night, but the timing wasn't appropriate. As Jackson neared the table, she nodded to Cynthia for the advice. "Have a safe journey home."

"Oh, we're not going home tonight. We're here in the hotel to make a weekend of it in Quebec City."

Polly inched her way toward Jackson with an exaggerated hobble about the shoes and grabbed his arm for support.

"I'll gladly carry you, Polly."

"No, no way. I'm walking out of my first Policeman's Ball with one of the finest. I'll not have a scrawny blister mar this evening."

In the limo, he slipped his arm around her. "Use my shoulder as your pillow. If traffic is good, we'll be home in an hour."

Polly's eyes opened again as the lights of Lac Maurice and the slowing of the car's engine stirred her.

"I'm sorry for sleeping all the way." Polly felt a stab of pain, wanting to ask him more.

At the door, she pulled herself up on her toes and waited for his kiss. From the limo, he watched that she was safely inside and gave a last wave as the door closed.

The vision of Jackson in the ballroom stayed in her mind until she drifted off, wishing he could be with her so she could comfort him.

At eight o'clock, Kate tapped at her door. "Polly, you awake?"

"Come in, Kate."

"Alright, sis. Tell me all about it."

She went directly to the dresser and picked up the rose corsage. "I wasn't sure if I was supposed to wait up for you."

Polly laughed. "It was like being a princess in a castle. He was a dashing gentleman and I was literally swept off my feet. I really like him, Kate."

"Then you hang in there and make sure he knows."

"He knows, I'm quite sure. But I don't want to smother him or rush the future."

"You're like Mom was with sentimental advice. Are you free to go into town for brunch? I was at a neat place with friends near Hanson Ridge that has a Sunday brunch—an antique place with a tea room."

"Let me jump in the shower. Is Tim home?"

"His door is closed. That usually means a late night."

"Is he okay, Kate? He has withdrawn from me lately, and I worry. I hope the ride-alongs work out. It brought him back to the old Tim, as he was so excited Monday night."

"I waited up for him, and we had a good talk about things."

"For fourteen, you're pretty smart. I'll leave a note on his door about family supper tonight."

"Put one right on his kitchen plate. He's sure to see that."

It was snowing when they left the house. Hank was in his driveway and rushed over waving his hands.

"Have you heard the news? There was a terrible fire last night. The Winslow house burnt to the ground."

Polly's face went white.

"Jackson! Oh, gracious no . . . and the Crawford family. Is everyone alright?"

"I don't know, Polly. Perhaps you should go in and turn on the TV news. I remember hearing that detective Tripp was seeing you. He has a room there, doesn't he?"

"Hank, I'm sick with worry. Thank you."

Kate was first in. Polly turned up the volume and sank into her father's armchair with her hand clasped to her heart.

Breaking News: This morning the fire department is extinguishing the last remnants of the Winslow fire off of Cricklecreek Road in Lac Maurice. Fortunately when the blaze started. No one was at home. The Crawfords had gone to Montreal for the weekend and have been contacted and are on their way back. First appearances indicate the fire may have been caused by an arsonist and began about one a.m. A neighbor noticed the smoke and called in the alarm. By the time the fire trucks were on sight, the house was fully engulfed.

Anyone noticing suspicious movement around the residence last night should call the police. A first examination indicates the fire began on the main floor and quickly spread to the second and third levels until the roof collapsed.

The Winslow House was the historic residence built by Clinton Weaver in the latter part of the 19th century. After the First World War, the Winslow family occupied the home until it was purchased by the Crawfords. Our local Historical Society was in the midst of an application to have the property classified as a Heritage Site.

"Kate, there's no mention of Jackson or any boarders. It said the fire started around one. When would he get home?"

"About that time."

They watched a video replay showing blackened timbers, a crumbled foundation, burnt out fixtures and part of a fireplace still standing. The entire house was demolished and the garage charred.

"They said no-one was home," Kate said.

Polly closed her eyes. "Nobody could survive that."

Sickened by even the thought that Jackson could be a victim, her thoughts spun wildly in her head. She couldn't bear that this Christmas could repeat the tragic loss of last year.

"This can't be. Dear God, I lost my parents last year and now this. I can't lose Jackson . . . I love him." The realization of her words jolted her upright, and she gripped the couch as she ran frantically to the wall phone to call Jackson's station.

"Hello, I just heard about the Winslow fire. I need to know about Jackson Tripp."

"Polly, this is Jackson. I'm okay."

A shudder of relief fell over her.

"What are you doing at the police station?"

"I have no home."

"We have a huge house and my parent's room hasn't had a guest for more than a year. Please come over and get rest and a shower. You're probably exhausted. You can sleep all day and we are having family supper tonight. Please say you will."

"Polly, it wouldn't be right."

"I don't care about gossip, only about you. I'll fret all day if you don't."

Finally, she heard a chuckle in Jackson's voice.

"Just one day. The station is trying to find me a hotel room somewhere, but with the holiday everything is full at the moment."

"What about the Crawfords?"

"We'll talk when I get there."

Polly watched at the window for his truck or a cruiser, then leaned against the front door waiting for a knock.

"Jackson!"

Polly flung open the door—there he was, looking tired but still wearing his tuxedo and looking handsome to her in his five o'clock shadow.

Assessing his beleaguered condition, she didn't ask a question. "Come upstairs and I'll show you where you can sleep. My father's clothes are exactly where he left them, and you can help yourself to anything you need. The room has its own private bath."

He threw his jacket on the floor and crashed on the bed dropping his shoes to the floor. Polly and Kate tip-toed downstairs.

"Bacon and eggs, I think." Polly immediately drew out her mother's cast iron fry pan and set the bacon to sizzle.

"I'll do coffee," Kate volunteered. "Should I set for two or three or four?"

"I think it's just us two, Kate," Polly said.

"What will Tim think when he comes down and Jackson is here in Dad's clothes?"

"I'll rely on his good sense of humor that all Perkins have," Polly said.

"He does look pretty good with that soot all over his face!"

12

"A house guest?" Tim said. It was close to noon when he came down, stunned by Kate's news to him of the Winslow fire.

"Yes. It's Jackson," Kate said. "Don't be surprised if he comes down looking a bit like Dad. He lost everything in the fire."

He perked up. "Jackson! That's awesome. But who would want to burn down the old Winslow house?"

"The news report said it was arson at around one a.m."

Tim's face went white, and Polly saw his agitation as his eyes darted back and forth.

"What's the matter, Tim? Do you know something?"

"No . . . no, I don't." His voice raised. "You're looking at me like I'm an accomplice or something."

Polly was speechless, reviewing the possibilities.

Tim grabbed a sandwich and was quickly out the door escaping from the inquisition.

"What would Mom and Dad have done?" Polly asked.

"Don't worry, he'll grow out of it. Can we do Christmas baking while we wait for Jackson? I'll get out that old recipe book and turn up the Christmas station for inspiration."

"While 'we' wait?" Polly laughed, both amused and gratified by Kate's reaction.

In no time, the counter was laden with trays of sugar cookies, jam thumbprints, lemon lace dainties, marshmallow chocolate clusters, peanut butter date balls rolled in coconut and Grandma Perkin's famous mincemeat tarts and gingerbread cake recipe with lemon sauce.

"That's the kind of Christmas comfort food we need," Kate said as she swallowed a peanut butter ball.

Polly had just put a ham in the oven for dinner when she heard footsteps on the stairs.

"Jackson! You're clean and refreshed—is it really you?"

"I slept like a log. The bed was much better than what I'm used to, and I helped myself to some of your Dad's clothes. We must be about the same height but I have an extra notch on my belt. The pants are a bit baggy."

"Turn around and I'll check you over," she teased. "Baggy has never looked better, and the plaid shirt and cable knit sweater have a Christmassy look. You look dashing."

"Is there a bakery in here? The smell drifted to my room."

"Almost," Kate said. "Did you realize that Christmas is only one week away?"

"Yes, of course. Sorry, but my mind is preoccupied with the Winslow house. I should call the station for an update. Have you heard any more news?"

"We've been busy in the kitchen," Polly confessed. "If you sit by the TV, I'll bring you a coffee."

"After a call." He sniffed the air. "I smell gingerbread."

With the kitchen cleaned up, the girls surrounded him by the TV to pepper him with questions.

"What do they know yet?" Kate asked.

"It appears intentionally started in the living room. There was a report earlier of several boys nearby that looked suspicious and may have been casing the house. Within half an hour a neighbor called in about smoke. I was on my way home when I saw flames on the horizon. It would have started about an hour before. I couldn't believe it was my own home. I'm not a pack rat, but everything I own was in my apartment."

Polly squeezed his hand. "I'm sorry. I can't imagine losing your home and all your belongings."

"There wasn't much for me and I can replace things. But poor Wayne and his family lost everything. They drove back from Quebec City early this morning and have gone to stay at Cynthia's parents. The kids were already there for the weekend while Wayne and Cynthia went to the ball."

"Is there anything we can do?" Kate asked.

"Because Wayne is on the police force, there will be a charity drive to help them recover some costs as insurance only covers so much. I'm sure they would appreciate any volunteer help to organize a benefit."

"I could round up some friends," Kate said. "We could plan something in the holidays; that's when folks are most charitable."

"Where's Tim?" Jackson asked.

"He went out in a huff," Kate tattled. Something bothered him about the fire and he didn't want to talk."

"May I use your phone again? I should check in at the station."

After a long, troubled conversation with his Lieutenant, Jackson returned with a solemn look.

"I have a uniform in the car. I'll change and go into the office. There's surveillance footage around the time of the fire, and they want to know if I recognize anyone in a group of boys that were noted in the area. It's now a full-fledged arson investigation."

Polly and Jackson locked in their puzzled thoughts, each thinking the other was holding back information. She was reluctant to persist or overstep.

He changed quickly and returned to Polly in the living room. "I'm sorry to leave . . . can we talk later?" At the door, he kissed her forehead.

"No apologies needed, Jackson. You have no obligation to tell me about your work." After she said it, the words stung her with reality.

No obligation to tell me.

Polly wished the facts were different. As the door closed, she felt a momentary loneliness, with a reminder of the past loss in her life. These walls that so often held so much joy seemed to be closing in around her.

With Kate off to town to shop, Polly curled up on an afghan her grandmother had made. A parade of cherished past times filled the room—times when the walls absorbed only joy and laughter.

On the radio, she listened to Boney M's new release, *Mary's Boy Child* and as her spirit revived, her toes became animated, wiggling and tapping to the music.

"Oh, my Lord," she hummed as she lit the logs on the hearth.

She recalled aunts and uncles arriving at their doorstep on Christmas Day, expecting kisses by reluctant children, with soft, fragile, old ladies smelling heavily of rose water, some with peculiar circles of rouge on their cheeks.

After the dinner plates were cleared for games for the kids, it was a day of jigsaw puzzles, Monopoly and crokinole with the cousins.

"And the time Santa, the familiar red elf himself, shocked Grandmother Perkins dipping her under the mistletoe. On one leg, with the other straight out, Grandma giggled and blushed at first, then hammed it up in the rollicking laughter, with exaggerated antics with her face and hair. I miss her so much. It was marvelous to watch the fascination on the faces of young cousins as they grasped to fathom where Santa had come from."

Polly's face then sobered up, remembering when a long-lost relative arrived at the door with a heartfelt greeting, wanting nothing in return.

"Mom and Dad always welcomed newcomers with open arms. What about those that are alone this Christmas? And what about Harris Winslow? He's a rejected cousin of sorts and through his own devices is down on his luck. In spite of the legal ramifications, he should be told of the demise of the Winslow house."

Beside the phone was Milton Marlborough's number.

"Good day, Milton. I want to follow up on the Harris Winslow suit. The facts were quite clear from our last discussion and I was expecting to receive some Release papers."

"As it is Christmas week, there is no urgency, Miss Perkins."

"There's an important new issue," she said. "The Winslow house had a fire last night. They say it was arson. As a courtesy, Harris should be notified. Would it be possible for me to contact him myself?"

Milton listened intently. "Arson, you say. I find this quite concerning, Ms. Perkins. May I have the case file number? I'd like to follow up with the investigators in this regard. However, it would be highly irregular if I gave you Mr. Winslow's personal contact."

Polly was confused. "I don't understand, he's my cousin."

Milton hesitated before speaking. "I've been having difficulty locating my client since he was notified that the claim was negated."

"That is peculiar," she said. "Can you fax me a current photo of Harris Winslow?"

"I see no harm in that and if his contact appears on the fax, I'll disclaim the source. I'll do it right away. And notify me of any new developments about the fire. Considering that Mr. Winslow cannot be located and his the anger he has expressed toward the Winslow descendants, we should be thorough."

At the kitchen table, Polly examined the faxed photo of Harris. She recalled a collection of black and white photos tied with twine in the document box, and thumbing through, she recognized a picture of her mother as a girl, with a gangly boy beside her.

"For his age now, he's prematurely bald but he has a sly smile, the kind of person you don't immediately trust. That's proven with his past frauds. Yet there is something familiar. No doubt in my childhood I would have crossed paths with him. But . . ."

Knowing something was wrong, she phoned Jackson and spoke directly to the point. "Is there any news about the arson case?"

"You know I can't discuss details with you. Why? Have you found new information?"

"Two scenarios trouble me, Jackson. I'm scared."

"Meet me at Sal's in half an hour."

Polly placed the photo in a brown envelope and left immediately for downtown. Hank was tinkering under the hood of his truck and Polly waved, but he obviously wanted to talk and stopped her at the end of the lane.

"Have they come to any conclusions about the fire?"

"Everyone in town will be curious," she said, "but I haven't heard any results yet."

Hank stammered. "I don't want to be the one telling tales, but one of the neighbors on Cricklecreek apparently saw some suspicious folks in the area before the fire."

"Would I be able to check that out, Hank? Which neighbor would that be?"

"Sure, Polly. Mrs. Simmonds, across the street in the brown brick house. You'll see her name on the gate."

"Thanks, Hank. I'll let you know if I find anything." She knew it was a lie, as any gossip about the fire would not be coming from her.

With a few minutes to spare, she swung by Cricklecreek Road. Mrs. Simmonds was collecting her mail when Polly pulled up.

"Good day, Mrs. Simmonds. It's a splendid day, isn't it? We'll keep our fingers crossed though for a White Christmas."

"Nice to see you, Polly. I'm sorry about the fire."

"My neighbor, Hank, said you might have seen some unusual folks around the area that night. Could you tell me a bit more about them?"

"Well, after those boys were causing a racket, a fellow driving an old Saab kept circling the block. Since it was dark, I assumed someone was lost so I sent Allan out to check. The fellow asked if it was the Winslow house."

"Can you describe him?"

"I gave what I could remember to the police. He was flashy and cocky and it was hard to tell how old he might have been. He had that premature balding hairline and a sneer I didn't like much."

"Thanks, Val, I appreciate the information. I'm supposed to meet a friend for coffee, so I'll be off. If I don't see you before, have a Merry Christmas!"

"Merry Christmas to you too, Polly."

Jackson was alone when she arrived at the café. From across the room, he looked anxious as he methodically rubbed his temple.

"Hi, Jackson."

"Polly, I can't be seen talking to you right now."

"I don't understand." She felt like she was falling off a cliff.

The somber look on his face remained. "For the next few days, I won't be in touch."

"Are you canceling the gala on Saturday at the Warner's? Or is it the arson case? You owe me an answer to both of those questions."

"I wouldn't cancel a date with you if my life depended on it."

Polly sighed her relief. "Thank you. I won't ask about the fire, but I have information I will run by you, off the record."

"Off the record? I'm a police officer, Polly."

She did her best, to sum up the claim against the Perkins estate and explain about Milton Marlborough and Harris Winslow.

"Have a look at this picture, Jackson. My neighbor, Hank, said a friend of his on Cricklecreek saw suspicious activity. I know there are reports that boys were pranking before the fire and I'm afraid Tim's name might come up. I know you'll do the right thing for Tim, whether it's helping him through a rough spot or eking a confession."

He listened without a reply.

"But it's after that," she continued. "Mrs. Simmonds gave an account to the police about the prowler driving a Saab."

Jackson raised his eyebrows, surprised what Polly knew.

She lifted the photo. "This is Harris Winslow and he has a motive. I believe he was seen in the area. I hope I am wrong and that we can find this lost relative, and maybe even bring him home for Christmas. But that's for you to find out."

"What are you asking?"

"Please review Mrs. Simmonds description again. The receding hairline, Saab, and an evil sneer."

"Thanks, Polly. This would answer a lot of questions and I'll check into the case. There is a second report of the same man. If it is Harris Winslow, I'll be sure to let you know."

Polly had finished her mission and rose to leave. He reached for her hand.

"Saturday, it's just you and me again."

13

From an outdoor vendor, she picked up poinsettias, holly, cranberries and a bag of Italian chestnuts, then visited Bittner's Emporium for table crackers and tea lights for her table setting as her store's stock was sold out. Inside Bittner's, she spotted Cynthia Crawford and squeezed through the crowd.

"Oh, Cynthia, how are you doing? I've been worried sick."

"We are quite comfortable at my parent's house over the holidays. I love Cricklecreek Road so we plan to rebuild on the same site once the insurance investigators have come to a settlement with us."

"Is there anything we can do to help?"

"We'll be fine, but thanks. I heard that the police force has found a room and board situation for Jackson over the holidays."

"That's good."

Polly was surprised by the news and wondered why Jackson hadn't mentioned it at the café.

Has the romance fizzled that quickly?

Jackson returned to the station with information to refocus the investigation away from the boys and onto this stranger cruising town in the Saab. In a corner office with partial wall dividers, he consulted with a pair of detectives working on forensics and the timeline.

"Cal, here's a photo of this man, Harris Winslow, late thirties. Last known address was in New York and he drives an older model Saab. Can you run a search on him, and verify with Mr. Simmonds, the witness, if this is the same person he saw that night?"

"This could be the break we need, Jackson. Where'd you get this?"

"It's not relevant to the investigation at this time."

"Jackson, if it's from your girl, we know that she has a connection to the old Winslow fortune."

"I don't know anything about a Winslow fortune, but if you are asking if the information came from Polly, does that matter?"

Wayne Crawford sauntered in at that moment.

"I overheard some discussions about my house. Come and talk to me. Tell me about this Harris person, Jackson."

Wayne was usually jovial, but today he was dead serious. He nodded to an isolated office and closed the door to discuss the circumstances.

"That's a coincidence and fits an outstanding piece. A week before the fire, a guy phone phoned saying the house was rightfully his. We wrote it off as a crank call."

The turn of events alarmed Jackson. "Wayne, I'm not so sure that Polly and the kids are safe right now. I'll talk to the Lieutenant about the risk, and perhaps I should return to the Perkins house to protect them. We can't wake up some morning finding that the Perkins place had been burnt to the ground too."

"If this man is indeed Harris Winslow, he appears to have a vendetta. Suddenly the case is becoming much more dangerous."

The Lieutenant agreed about police protection and phoned Polly to inform her. "We'll put your address and the antique shop on our patrol routes, Polly, but if you're in agreement, you'll be safer if Jackson Tripp could reside there when off duty for your protection. The department will compensate you for room and board until the arson matter is resolved. Furthermore, if you come across anything else about this Winslow fellow, call us immediately."

"Officer Tripp is absolutely welcome, Lieutenant Thorne, but I'll not hear of compensation. Be assured of our full cooperation."

Polly hung up the phone, relieved that Tim's name hadn't come up in the conversation, but it nagged at her that he had withdrawn his confidences.

Jackson was tortured by a desire to rescue this family as his own—to be a big brother to Kate and Tim, to guide Tim to find a fulfilling path in life and to cradle Polly with love. These were new feelings to him.

His youth in Hanson Ridge had no foundation but had mostly memories of uncertainty and abandonment. As a young boy, he pretended to be strong to help his brother while his family unit disintegrated.

His father instigated constant arguments of resentment with his mother in front of the two boys.

"Meredith, I'll never be able to offer you a mansion and I don't like you working there. You don't even use your married name, but go under your maiden name, Carver. How do you think that makes me feel?"

"Clarence, I chose you. You came to my rescue and I will always be grateful for that."

"You'll never be able to convince me of that. You were pregnant when I married you . . . I did it out of pity. I demand that you quit working at the fancy house!"

"If that's what you really want, Clarence, I'll quit."

His father quietly moved away leaving his mother to support two young boys. Christmases were cold and empty, seldom with a tree or gifts. The reality at home pained him, but he told his schoolmates of fabricated happy times and vacations.

At his last Christmas with his brother, Jarvis, they lined up at the soup kitchen in a neighboring town for a meager meal.

When his mother found out, she was enraged. Jarvis challenged her for the first time and it ended with him slamming the door for the last time. Soon after, his mother disappeared with a man she'd met in a local bar and never returned.

Jackson never told anyone about his fragile youth, not even Wayne. Instead, he took on extra shifts over the holidays, avoiding Christmas and easing his anguish. It was rewarding enough to see others with families enjoy the holiday.

Jackson had two lives—the restlessness of a homeless situation and the façade of a solid citizen longing for a story-book family. Beneath it, was a desire to feel loved and give back in return. Buoyed up by his reflection of Tim's trusting face and Kate's quiet admiration, he was resolved to fill the void in the family's lives.

Waiting for Wayne in the cruiser, Jackson watched the lines of children at the town hall gingerbread house, and beyond it, families of all ages flocking to the live nativity scene. A pair of boys Jackson recognized were chasing each another in and out of the stable. The taller one was responsible for watching two sheep grazing in the yard.

As Wayne got in the car, Jackson said, "Wait . . . watch this. He's getting on the sheep."

The windows were closed, but Wayne shouted, "Don't do that, kid. Don't get on the sheep!"

"Too late." The escapade was underway and the unsuspecting animal reeled with the kid on his back. Kicking his heels high only increased the boys' thrill and delight.

"Yippee-ki-yai!" they roared with delight.

Mr. Heard's border-collie was frantic trying to prevent the abuse of his charges. Jackson and Wayne raced toward the chaos to hold back the cheering crowd.

"Dennis! Get off!" Jackson yelled.

The sheep's eyes were wild as he bucked, and as the people moved closer, Jackson feared a catastrophe. On the second go-round, he swooped the boy off the sheep's back by the scruff of his collar.

"Let me go, we were just havin' fun," Dennis cried.

Jackson remained controlled. "The Church provided this for a reason—but not for riding."

In seconds, the farmer, Mr. Heard, was there to console the sheep, now whining at the traumatic imposition.

"Calm down, Lucy. It'll be alright."

The farmer patted the victim's head and talked softly in its ear. He continued to stroke it until her breathing relaxed.

"Dennis, you owe Mr. Heard an apology," Jackson said. "The police station is across the road, with a security camera fixed on the Church. Any misbehaving and we know exactly who the culprit is."

. . . We know exactly who the culprit is . . .

Jackson was no longer thinking of Dennis and the sheep but flashed to the Winslow house. "Wayne, maybe residents on Cricklecreek Road have security cameras."

From the car, Wayne called the detectives' desk.

"I'll check," Cal said. Two or three security firms have service in the area."

"We taking a ride over there to check something out." Jackson disappeared to recruit his partner.

"Come on, Wayne, some sleuthing to do."

"Sleuthing . . . we're going to be sleuths? That's a new one," Wayne chortled.

"I've been putting a few clues together. I have a feeling the mischievous local boys have nothing to do with the fire, but that it was merely the coincidence of timing. It's the stranger in the Saab that warrants our suspicion."

"You think he's the one that called my house?"

"I do, and if he were so bold as to burn your house down, he has a vendetta and that could possibly endanger the

Perkins. This is confidential, but since it's your house that got burnt, I'll tell you. The Harris fellow had filed a claim of right against the previous owners of Winslow house."

At the corner of Cricklecreek, Wayne pointed at a market with a lone pair of gas pumps.

"Slow down; this is the corner of Cricklecreek. He would have come this way from downtown, especially if he's new to the area."

Parking in the lot, Jackson found cameras at the pumps and front door. As he cased the vantage points outside, Wayne went in to talk to the clerk who began collecting a stack of tapes from the manager's office.

"Beta? You're kidding!"

The clerk laughed. "Mr. Newell says you don't need to fix something that ain't broke. Whatever you're looking for will be on there, I have no doubts."

"Thank him for us. We'll return these after our review."

Continuing on Cricklecreek toward the Winslow house, they noted security signs at a number of residences.

The remains of the house were cordoned off with plywood boards. A six-foot fence around the yard with a yellow tape warned of the crime scene.

"The rest of the street is still quite pretty with so many houses having Christmas lights. Did I tell you that we're going to rebuild once the insurance money comes through?"

"I'm glad to hear that, Wayne, and so will the neighbors."

"Hopefully the insurance company will be efficient and we'll quickly determine who the culprit is. It appears that the offender broke in before he lit the fire. We had a safe in the parlor. He couldn't open it but it appears he tried to drag it out first."

"For Polly's sake, I hope her cousin was not involved."

"It isn't looking good."

14

Polly whistled a line of *Rudolf* as she unpacked a shipment of Christmas stock. The best time to get this work done was on Monday when shops were closed. She was one of the faithful few that remained open and knowing the shopping traffic would be diminished, she would spruce up her displays. She tried to keep her mind off of Jackson.

Tim had kept to himself more than usual but tonight he would resume his ride-along schedule. That was a relief to Polly, as he'd be re-energized and optimistic after it and would likely talk more openly afterward.

I want to see him more involved in the family.

Polly cranked up the Christmas music and crawled into the window to turn on the train set. The late afternoon sky was dark and she glanced out at the Christmas lights that reflected on merchants' windows.

Suddenly she jumped to her feet.

"It's the Saab . . . driving slowly past. Is it my imagination or is he casing my shop? Is he peering into my window? It's too late to turn off the train and it's obvious that I'm in here."

She locked the door and turned the lights and music off. Staying low, she made her way to the phone on the counter.

An unfamiliar voice answered the phone.

"Officer, this is Polly Perkins. I'm working in my store, Treasure Box. I have a connection with the Winslow fire and with the man in the Saab. He's driving back and forth in front of my store right now. Would you send a cruiser by?"

"Stay where you are, Miss Perkins. A unit is on its way."

On the floor, she was out of sight as she waited. She froze at a knock at the door, watching the flicker of a flashlight. With her heart pumping, she crept to the window. Squinting into the darkness, she sighed at the sight of Wayne and Jackson. Tim, on a ride-about, waited in the cruiser.

"Thanks for coming! Sorry if I overreacted, but the sight of the Saab scared me."

As she studied Jackson's concern, she downplayed the pathetic fear she'd felt.

Wayne offered his noble words, "Better to be cautious than caught in a dangerous situation."

"Pack up here for the night, Polly. We'll follow you home and make sure the Saab isn't around," Jackson said gently. "In fact, we can drive you home in the cruiser. I'll drop you and Tim at the house, and tomorrow I'll bring you in when I go to work."

At the Maple house, he escorted Polly and Tim to the front door.

"Tim, keep an eye out and call me if you see him."

"It'll be alright, Polly," Tim said. "We'll see you're never alone until this is resolved. Jackson explained to me about the Winslow case. Be assured I have nothing to do with the fire and take me at my word that I'll look out for you."

Suddenly Tim seemed taller and more of a man than she had remembered. "Thank you, Tim. It's always good to have a man in the house."

"Did the Lieutenant call you?" Jackson asked. "My shift is over in an hour."

"Yes, we're expecting you. The spare key is in a tin under the mailbox. Keep it for as long as you need."

Polly lingered, feeling limp but heartened by his presence.

"Have faith in me and I won't let you down," he promised, then leaned in with a soft kiss.

Knowing she wouldn't sleep, she went to her mother's closet to peruse the evening gowns, looking for one in particular.

"The pearly pink one with chiffon sleeves . . . you always looked like a princess, Mom, wearing it with your silver slippers."

As she thumbed through the hangers to find it, she held up others to examine. "After all it will be a Christmas Eve Ball, and there's nothing wrong with looking festive. Cynthia was a vision in Montreal wearing red."

She removed an emerald green silk gown to hold up in front of the mirror. It had a full skirt and see-through sleeves with crusted beads at the cuffs and waistband.

"This is the one, and the scooped neckline is just begging for Grandmother Perkins' diamond necklace."

She slipped into it, then a pair of silver sling-backs that highlighted the jewelry and the beaded pouch bag.

"I must tell Jackson the colors I've chosen."

Carrying her wardrobe to her room, she resigned herself to a good night's sleep.

Her eyes closed to a vision of dancing at Warner's Ball in the magic silver slippers. Her dreams floated her down the Cinderella staircase with Prince Jackson at her side. The orchestra lured them to the dance floor and she drifted away to a heavenly slumber.

In the morning, she could smell the coffee halfway down the stairs.

"Mmm . . . it's just what I need." She rounded the corner expecting Kate but instead found Tim at the table with Jackson.

"Morning, Sunshine! I was awake early and picked up some of Sal's fresh baked muffins for breakfast."

"If you keep this up, we might not let you leave." He looked up, about to speak, but held back the quip on his tongue.

"My shift doesn't start 'til afternoon. If you need anything done in the house, Polly, I'm ready and willing."

"Really, I could use some help. I have a fresh turkey on order if you could pick it up." She leaned for a kiss as she filled his cup.

"We'll also need champagne and orange juice for Christmas morning and a load of firewood from Hank's Garage."

"Come and sit with us," he said. "When you're ready, I'll take Kate and Tim to school and drop you at the store. Can you meet me at the diner for lunch?"

"You're spoiling us, you know."

"I haven't had a family to spoil in a long time."

"Well, you lucked out . . . it seems that we're all up for adoption."

"Yeah, Jackson," Tim said. "I could use another man in the house, to balance the scales so to speak."

"Enough sweet talk, round up your bags and get in the truck."

With the kids dropped, she asked, "Did you find out anything new about Harris?"

"We got security footage from the gas station and the neighbors and we're tracking his movements that day."

"Have you found him?"

"Not in Lac Maurice, so we're sending a car to surrounding towns to check motels."

"Although he scares me, I feel sorry that he could feel so much hate at this time of year."

She opened the Treasure Box door to a scent of eucalyptus, bayberry and cinnamon spice, muddled with vanilla bean-scented candles.

"Morning, Soph. What a weekend! Smells in here like you're making up a wassail bowl full of cheer."

Sophia poked her face out from the back room. "There was a delivery as soon as I got here, also a box of holly with berries that I put in the cooler for you."

"I ordered that from Montreal. We always had sprigs of it decorating our turkey platters at Christmas. It's an old tradition Grandmother insisted on."

As Sophia talked on in the background, Polly's mind flashed to her memories of her grandmother and the wonderful stories she had told of her ancestors.

I will always honor my family and those that came before me including the original innkeeper of Lac Maurice, Ichabod Perkins. No one left his inn on an empty stomach. His hospitality was known to be abundant then and it will be now. Christmas is the time to bring in the fold.

Sophia's voice tuned in to Pally again. "We received a back-up shipment of table crackers. Did we happen to order double?"

"No, but we're happy to have it. Put a wooden basketful by the front and they'll be gone in no time. And set aside a box for me too."

"These are especially lovely, guaranteed to have the best prizes."

"No Christmas feast is complete without crackers, and my father always made us wear those awful paper hats."

"This morning, the Food Bank folks came by," Sophia said. "They took away the can donation basket and left a new one. It's sad that folks still go hungry at Christmas. We assume everyone has family somewhere and a place to go for Christmas dinner, but some people might feel shame and not let on they are alone for the holidays."

"Sophia, do you know anything about the Tripp family from Hanson Ridge? I know so little about a man I care so much for."

Sophia hesitated then spoke reluctantly.

"My aunt was a live-in maid in a grand house out there about ten years ago. I vaguely remember her mentioning the Tripp name, and that her boss had called Social Services on the parents for abusing their children. I can't tell you any details. I never thought to connect that story with your Jackson."

"There must be another Tripp family. Jackson is proud of his background."

Sophia didn't say more.

It's better to leave things unsaid than say the wrong thing that you can't correct.

15

As she approached Jackson's booth at Sal's, he stood. He'd been watching from the window, and his brown-green eyes came alive at her sight.

"You're so tall and handsome in your dark navy uniform and polished boots," she said and squeezed in beside him. "How was your morning?"

A half-smile crossed her face, wondering about the truth behind this man who had captivated her and given her hope for the future.

"I'm fine, Jackson. I'd like to know all about you. About today, yesterday and tomorrow."

"That's a tall order."

"It's time for that, isn't it?"

The waitress arrived with coffee and Polly picked the daily special to avoid the delay.

"What do you want to know about me?"

His hand gently eased back, but she held on tightly. "No, Jackson, you can't pull away from me anymore."

"Well, I told you my family is away for Christmas and that I grew up in Hanson Ridge."

"Yes, you've told me that. But there's something else you are concealing. I've seen pain cross your face when we reminisce about good times and old memories. Who are your parents? Where's your brother?"

The words stabbed at him and his eyes returned to the window. "You go right to the jugular don't you."

"If it makes it easier for you to tell me, I'll give you a summation of what I know."

Surprised, he nodded without a word.

"You did grow up in Hanson Ridge. Your great-aunt was Wilhelmina Hanson, a mysterious character in the Winslow case, but your father abandoned his family when you were a teenager. Your mother struggled to raise two boys on her own but failed and turned to alcohol. Your brother had a confrontation for some unknown reason and left home. You haven't seen your family for Christmas in years, or any other time of the year."

Jackson's face was white.

"I'm sorry, Jackson, but I need to let you into my life. All of you—and that's the here and now. But everyone comes with a past. I care too much now."

An unexpected relief overcame Jackson and he turned back to her.

"Thanks, Polly, for opening the door. Yes, everything you said was right except that Wilhelmina Hanson was my grandmother, not my aunt. I'm always on the lookout for Jarvis, hoping to see him again one day. I received news some years back that my mother had died in prison and I regretted not being there for her or at her funeral."

"I understand, Jackson. When Mom and Dad died last year it was unbearable. It's natural to reflect on yourself to seek out what you might have done better . . . to have said a goodbye and reassurance of your love. I've learned that I have nothing to feel guilty about. You're not alone, Jackson. You have us behind you."

The lunch plates arrived but they both picked at it, neither with an appetite. With refilled coffee, Jackson's demeanor returned to that of a policeman. "I want to tell you some news about your cousin."

"Yes, please tell me."

"We're almost one hundred percent certain that Harris Winslow was the driver of the Saab. It's been collaborated by video and eyewitness accounts."

"Where is he?"

"At a motel in Lansdowne and we have him under surveillance. I'll go there this afternoon with one of the detectives to confront him."

She listened thoughtfully then abruptly raised her hand. "I understand what I'm about to say comes out of left field . . . but could I tag along? I want to meet Harris. Perhaps he feels some remorse, but nonetheless, it seems I am his only relative that cares right now."

Jackson's eyebrows raised. "What would your intention be?"

"I'd like him to know that he is forgiven."

"That would not be the position of the police."

"So is it at all possible?"

"You have a kind heart, Polly, but I can't see the Lieutenant agreeing to that."

"I understand. But let me know what happens."

"Sure. I'll be at the house after seven tonight. We'll talk then."

Jackson walked her out and before they went their own ways, he pulled her back.

She closed her eyes, enjoying this moment in his arms but opened them at the sound of Wayne's voice from the cruiser to claim his partner.

Entering the shop, Polly was surprised to see Cynthia Crawford at the counter, chatting with Sophia.

"Hello, Polly. After we spoke, it occurred to me that you lost a historic connection from the fire. You must have known the house as a child."

"I do have memories. It was just a house, but I'm grateful you gave me that precious box last week. It's been an eye-opener, to say the least. Did you see we got in a new shipment of table crackers, Cynthia? I'm sorry we were sold out last time."

"I would adore a pack of those for my parents' Christmas table. But before I get off track . . . I donated a box of military souvenirs and documents to the militia museum in Montreal. You might want to visit sometime and see if any of it belongs to your ancestors."

"I'll do that. Now again for the crackers, do you have a color theme for their Christmas table?"

"I'm partial to those red and gold flocked ones, but I'm easy to please. Ooh, those are delightful, but I'll need more than one box. Better do the green and red ones too. I must say it smells marvelous in here, that aroma of cider and cinnamon spice. It's magical and nostalgic."

"I feel that same way." She hugged Cynthia. "If I don't see you before, have a Merry Christmas."

With a customer lull, Sophia gently pressed her, "And how was lunch? Tell me."

"Each time with Jackson is special. He's a puzzle for sure. At the Policeman's Ball, Cynthia cautioned me not to dig up old wounds, but you know me, Soph. If you warn me off, it just peaks my curiosity further."

She clasped her hands together. "And I want to help Jackson find the happiness of a family at Christmas that he's been denied."

"If you ask me, you two are the perfect couple."

"Since my parents died, I never thought about meeting a man and building a future. I assumed I'd focus on Tim and Kate 'til they were out of college, to put them in the forefront and wait it out. Then one day, this handsome man walks into Sal's. I know the exact moment when he plucked at my heartstrings. I'd have an empty hole in my heart now if things didn't work out."

"When your father worked with us in the shop, he always gave us sage advice about life. He warned us not to rush the future, but cherish each day as a new day and look for the best in everyone," Sophia recounted.

"You're right . . . and in every encounter. I can almost hear his voice as you said that."

At the end of the day, the roads were clear, and on an impulse, Polly headed out towards Lansdowne, about twenty minutes down the road. Passing the Lac Maurice town limits, she wondered if Jackson had already encountered Harris Winslow at his motel.

"What am I doing? Jackson asked me to stay away. He was going on official police business. I have no right to interfere."

Slowing her foot on the gas, she pulled down a farmer's pasture lane to turn back as there was enough room on the gravel shoulder. Waiting for a traffic break, she saw the oncoming police cruiser heading back to town, with Jackson driving. She held her breath as it passed.

At the side of the road, she let the engine idle for ten minutes as she sorted out her thoughts, then merged back into traffic toward home.

Panic struck her almost immediately and her heart raced at a sudden predicament.

"The Saab is several cars in front."

She slowed to let a car pass. "I'll follow him. It's doubtful that he knows what my car looks like, or even me for that matter."

Dusk was falling when she reached the town limits, and she had difficulty keeping it in sight but knew it by its broken rear brake light.

The Saab eased its way slowly down Cricklecreek Road, then returned to the main road toward Maple.

"I can't stop at a phone booth to call the police or I'll lose him. I'll stay back."

He slowed in front of the Perkins house, then pulled onto the shoulder in a holding position.

"No doubt Kate or Tim will be in the house. I can't let Harris Winslow approach them. The Christmas tree lights are on, so it must be Kate downstairs."

From a distance, she assessed her options. "I can go on further to Hank Moffatt's house. He should be home."

She eased into his lane. "Ah, his truck is there."

Running to the front door, she pounded rapidly, and Hank was there in an instant.

"Hank, call the police! It's an emergency!"

"Come in, Polly."

"No, Hank. Call now. Every minute is life and death. Tell them the Saab is in front of my house. I think my brother and sister may be at home."

Although Hank didn't know the whole story, he knew enough, and he shouted to his wife who was behind him now.

"Barbara . . . Barb, call the police. The Saab is in front of Perkins' house."

Polly's thoughts were still racing, how to get to Kate and Tim before they opened the door to Harris Winslow.

"There's no knowing what he might do to Kate or Tim. I have to get to them."

"There are bushes at the back," Hank said. "I've dodged them from my hunting days. Stay here. I'll take my rifle and go around the back of the barn. I can get to your place without him seeing me."

"I'm coming with you, Hank."

"No, there's no point in putting yourself at risk."

Seeing the fury on Polly's face, he gave up his resistance. "Okay, but stay directly behind me and follow my lead, alright?"

"Yes . . . stay behind."

The snow was deep behind the barn as the shelter overhang had preserved recent weeks of snowfall. Hank grabbed a pair of snowshoes from the rack at the back and forged across behind the two houses.

"Can you sneak in the back of the house without being seen?" Hank asked.

"Sure can. I used to shinny off the roof from my window as a kid when my parents told me I couldn't go to the movies. There's a metal utility ladder that pulls up and down. I can get to the upper balcony off the master bedroom and I have a trick to wiggle the lock free."

"I'll stand guard by the back of your garage. The police should be here any minute."

The icy, retracting ladder shivered as she climbed to the eavestrough at the base of the balcony. Over the top, she saw that the Saab was still there. She wiggled onto the balcony, and with a few scrapes and bruises, she crawled to the balcony door.

She tiptoed down the dark hall. Kate looked up in alarm from her homework.

"Kate, stay in your room and down from the window. There's a prowler in the yard. The police are on their way."

16

Harris cowered low in his car, anxiously spying the house through a pair of pocket binoculars. His shoulders were pulled up high towards his ears, yet it was obvious that he was fuming and glaring with the anger he harbored for being denied. He muttered to himself how unjust the inheritance laws were.

That Perkins girl is doing her best to keep me from collecting my payout. I'll case the house and track where she goes. Marlborough told me she was shrewd but just wait and see. I'll have my way!

If Polly had seen his seething stare, it would have sent chills up her spine.

Jackson and his partner arrived without a siren and pulled up behind the parked vehicle with only a single beep to announce their authority on the scene. Wayne paced around the side of the vehicle and recorded the license number then tapped on the driver's window.

With no choice, Winslow got out and placed his hands on the hood. Sneering with resentment, he took a look back to see if the residents were watching his humiliation.

"Open your trunk, Winslow!" Wayne demanded.

"You got a search warrant? I haven't done anything wrong." His fists and teeth were clenched and angry spit spewed from his words.

"We don't need one to follow up on suspicious activity. We had that discussion already in Lansdowne, remember, Harris? You were warned to stay away from Lac Maurice and in particular, the Perkins house. And here you are, not half an hour later!"

Winslow didn't budge to open the trunk.

Jackson reached in for the keys from the ignition and pressed the trunk opener. Stashed in a pile were three gasoline jerry cans, oiled rags, and a box of tools.

Jackson was livid. "Arson evidence!" He grabbed for Harris's neck and Wayne intervened.

"Take it easy. The backup will be here in a minute. We haven't yet read Mr. Winslow his rights."

"Yeah, you got no right to touch me, copper!"

A second and third cruiser arrived as they cuffed Harris, and turning him over it to one of the backup cops, Jackson raced for the house for Polly.

He charged up onto the veranda, almost knocking over Hank who held a firm stance with his hunting rifle by his side, blocking access to the door.

"Whoa, do you have a permit for that Hank?"

"Sure do, but you don't want to waste your time about that, Jackson." Hank gave a no-nonsense wink as Jackson ran inside.

Waiting with Kate in her room, Polly looked the worse for wear with a forehead goose egg and a gash from her confrontation with the eaves. A shard of metal had torn her blouse and gouged her upper arm. The ladder had been more cumbersome than she recalled from her youth.

"Are you alright?"

Police lights were flashing outside, and seeing the gathering of Jackson's peers on the embankment, she reached for his hand rather than fall into his arms.

He could feel her trembling. "Don't stand up. It's all okay now."

"I'm so glad you're here now. What was Harris doing at our house? Surely he didn't really mean any harm to us?"

Her eyes looked to him for reassurance and she raised herself up supported by his arm.

"I insist on going outside to watch."

"Only to the veranda," he said. "Away from any contact with Harris Winslow."

A news van was on the street, with a young reporter and a cameraman circling the police with questions. Getting only sparse yeses and mostly no-comment answers, she spied Polly on the porch. Her camera was live.

"Miss Perkins, can you tell me what happened here this evening? Do you know the man in the vehicle? Who is he and why is he being arrested?"

Hank looked from Jackson to Polly to Wayne. Crossing his arms over his chest, he stepped out in front, with the persona of a guard dog with raised hackles.

"Excuse me, Ma'am, but Miss Perkins is still in shock. Perhaps you could come back tomorrow."

Jackson said, "Did you get a statement from Officer Crawford just now?"

"Yes, but I have questions for Miss Perkins."

"We have no police comment yet, but you can call the detachment in a few hours. Detectives will be assigned to the case and it is your right to follow-up. For now, you are being asked to vacate the Perkins property."

With a shrug, she trod back to the flashing police lights for on-air footage.

"Polly, let's go inside." Jackson took her elbow then turned back.

"Hank, put your rifle away before the other officers see you with it . . . but most of all, thanks for coming to Polly's aid. We need you to make a statement to the police."

"Can you stay?" Polly asked inside. "Do you have to go back with Wayne?"

"You know I'll stay. I couldn't leave you as a damsel in distress."

In the hallway, she moved closer to let his arms surround her. "Thank you. Thank you, Jackson."

Kate eased herself down the stairs. "Is the coast clear?"

Polly smirked at the image of Kate hiding out in her room all this time. "Coast is clear, Kate!" Jackson assured.

"What's happening? Why are all the police cars outside?"

"We need a pot of coffee," Polly said. "Then we'll have a long talk in the living room."

"Where's Tim?" Jackson asked. "He should know."

"I haven't seen him since this morning. Maybe barricaded in his room with his Atari games."

"Do you mind if I check?"

Jackson mounted the staircase and tapped. "Tim, are you there? It's me, Jackson. Can we talk?"

He heard soft shuffling but no reply. "Tim, something important happened today that you need to know about. Please come out."

Tim's voice was gruff. "I'm going to take a shower . . . I'll be down in five minutes."

"We'll wait. It's important family business."

Assembled in the living room, Jackson began to relay the day's events and the implications to the family.

"Polly knows some of this. But you . . . Kate and Tim. You should be included in this matter."

Tim showed an uncharacteristic, sudden concern. "You look pretty serious, Jackson."

"A man named Harris Winslow, a distant cousin, made a financial claim against the Winslow house. It was a bogus claim of a lost inheritance, but there's a long and complicated background to the story. His claim was denied, but the man was down and out on his luck and the news enraged him.

"Last Saturday, he was in Lac Maurice and neighbors saw him near the Winslow house before the fire. At this point, he's the suspected arsonist. The neighbors also reported a group of boys causing a raucous."

Jackson paused to look at Tim.

"We don't believe they were involved at all in the fire. You're off the hook, Tim, but I'd still like to talk to you later in private. If anything in your memory can provide the tiniest clue, it will be helpful."

Tim nodded. "What happened today?"

"Harris Winslow was seen several times this week driving the Saab that was yielded outside a few minutes ago."

Jackson took a slow sip from his cup, allowing time to absorb the news.

"Why was the Saab at our house?" Kate asked.

"Your grandmother comes from the Winslows that once owned the Cricklecreek house. Harris tracked his surviving relations to the Perkins household and launched a vendetta. We've had an extra patrol by your house for the last few days. Today, when arrested, he had gasoline and other equipment to commit arson. We believe he intended to burn your house as well."

"This can't be true!" Tim said.

"I'm afraid it is. At this moment he's in custody at the jailhouse pending a hearing. The immediate level of danger has been eliminated and it would seem that you are all safe now."

Polly added, "Jackson will be staying here for protection until the case is resolved."

"Besides, it's Christmas and I don't have any other place to be. I told Polly about my childhood today. My parents and my brother have been gone for some time. I'm grateful to be among the Perkins family for Christmas."

"I'm happy that you've put your feelings in the open," Polly said. "And proud."

Kate added, "I'm glad you're here as part of our family this Christmas. You're welcome for as long as you need."

"I could use an older brother too," Tim said. "If you don't mind."

"That's important to me too, Tim. My brother struggled with life in general, then walked out in fury from a silly argument and disappeared into the world. I've searched for him through Montreal and Quebec and other towns around. His name's Jarvis and I miss him very much. He's about five years older than you, Tim."

Polly moved closer on the sofa. "I can't imagine how painful Christmas has been for you without him."

"Thank you, Perkins family, but aren't you all starved about now? It's almost nine o'clock!"

Kate jumped up and disappeared. "Gosh, I forgot. A meatloaf is on a timer in the oven." As Polly rose to help, Jackson stopped her.

"Polly, you've had a rough day. Stay here and I'll give Kate a hand."

"You're lucky, Mom, he's a great guy eh?"

Polly heard the slip of the tongue.

"Thanks, Tim, you're a great one too." He squirmed at the compliment.

"I think I should get some firewood from the garage."

Left alone, Polly slid down onto the floor with her legs beneath her and pulled out a handful of pictures from the diary box.

"Oh, here's one of the Winslow family. It's Mom and Harris together. He was loved by his family and they would be pained to know what has happened," she muttered. "Especially at Christmas. There he sits in a jail, assuming no one cares. He does have a family and it seems that we are it."

She was struck again with a thought.

"It's what Mom would want me to do. I'm sure she must have had happy memories of family times with Harris."

She called the family together including Jackson. "You must hear this idea!"

At the round kitchen table, Polly broached her plan, boosted by her heart and a desire to right the world. She was welling with family pride as she shared it.

"Don't shoot me down too quickly, but I was thinking about Christmas and our family. In the pictures, I was reminded that Harris is a Winslow and was loved by his family.

"Parents never lose love for a child—it's unconditional and they love their children equally. Mom wouldn't want her cousin Harris to spend Christmas in a jail."

"What are you trying to say, Pol?" Jackson asked.

"You are working Christmas Day and thankfully you'll take a break and come for dinner. I'm wondering if we could arrange for Harris to join us, while in your custody, of course. It's the compassionate thing to do, isn't it?"

"The arsonist?" Tim said.

"Yes. Our relative that needs help."

Jackson paused in contemplation.

"I understand your motivation and it's a very generous suggestion. Harris is a suspected criminal and undeserving, and as you say it would show compassion. Don't get your hopes up, but I'll speak with the Lieutenant to call the Captain. However, be prepared that it will likely be rejected."

His thoughts went to his brother Jarvis, wondering where he was and where he would spend Christmas. His heart pounded, imagining his own blood being down and out of their luck and left homeless with disregard by society.

Wherever Jarvis could be, Jackson hoped that even one person would think kindly on him.

Polly said, "Would it help if I came with you to make the plea? After all, legally he is still my cousin."

"Let me think on that. I'll let you know before I go in tomorrow for my shift."

17

Before going up for the night, Polly returned to the veranda to survey the scene. The tow truck had left serious ruts removing the Saab, but otherwise, the threat and any inkling of today were gone. As dusk fell, the crust of the snow now had a quiet sparkle that reflected the stars.

"I learned a valuable lesson today, that forgiveness and love are essential to happiness. I can't begrudge this relative with nothing when we are blessed with so much."

Jackson was watching from the open doorway and joined her.

"Here we are standing under the mistletoe. Pretend I'm dressed in a Santa suit and I'm going to dip my girl," he smirked.

"You want to dip me?"

"Sure do."

Polly came near enough that she felt his breath on her neck. Then even closer, she sensed the beating of his heart beating and the warmth of his face against hers. His arms tightened around her and his lips softly touched hers until they were both embraced in a passionate kiss.

With one hand on her back, he leaned her backward. Without breaking the kiss, she allowed herself to swoon into the dip.

Just as Grandma Perkins did, she bent one leg underneath for support with the other pointing straight out. Polly found the escape quite comfortable and gave an exaggerated groan when he swayed her back onto two feet.

"We did that pretty well!" Jackson muttered and kissed her again.

"Polly Perkins, I've fallen in love with you."

Still embraced, she laid her head on his shoulder. "Jackson Tripp, I've fallen in love with you too."

Jackson turned on the Marconi to a mellow station and the two swayed to 50's music, absorbed in each other. An hour passed without notice until Tim burst in the door past midnight.

When she woke up, she was filled with giggles and thoughts of romance. It was Friday and tomorrow would be Warner's Ball. She sprung to her feet and dressed quickly to get down to see her prince.

Jackson and Tim were at the table in conversation, and she went directly to Jackson, kissing his cheek.

"Gosh, you two! Why don't you just get married?" Tim laughed.

"Listen, pal," Jackson said. "We need a man to man talk. Tim, can I take you for lunch today?"

"Sure, school is done for the holiday. I can meet you at any time.

"The rib place on Temple Street? I can be there at noon."

Jackson hadn't looked at Polly since Tim's marriage comment. He rose and went to the staircase and called out, "Kate are you up? I need to talk to you."

Sleepily, she drifted down in her housecoat. "Can't a girl sleep in on the holidays?"

"I guess I wasn't thinking, Kate."

She pried her eyes open with her fingers for effect. "You wanted me for some reason?"

"Yes, I do. I want to take you Christmas shopping with me. I could use your help, then we'll have tea at the Patisserie de Soleil."

"Me?" Kate winked at Polly and dashed upstairs.

"I'm here listening to every word," Polly moaned. "Am I invisible?"

"I was saving the best for last."

"Out with it then. I'm feeling a bit left out."

"I'll drive you to work and we'll talk in the car."

"If we go early, we can grab a coffee at Sal's."

In Jackson's truck, Polly waited for an announcement about Harris, but they were almost at Sal's before he uttered a word. Kate kept silent.

"Polly, I will give the Harris option a try, I promise. But there's no need for you to come. I've saved frugally since I've been working and I could put up bail for Harris if it comes to that."

Polly was stunned by his generous offer.

"It shouldn't be your burden to bear. He's my cousin. I'm sure I could get some funds from the bank."

"I tossed all night, thinking about it, and I feel better than I have in years. It's what I want to do."

"I know you want my best interests. See what the Captain says."

Sal's was hopping when they entered. "Have a seat," Peg called from the till. "Kate, your new brown Christmas parka is perfect. I heard about it from some ladies that stopped in here yesterday."

She picked up a coffee decanter. "What will it be today?"

"Depends. What's fresh out of the oven?" Jackson asked.

"Cinnamon buns are hot," Peg said. "Nice and sticky."

"Sold."

"Ooh, your sticky buns are the best. Me too," Kate added. "And a blueberry bran muffin, Peg."

"Hey, Kate—I had an idea. You're out of school tomorrow for the holidays, aren't you? How about earning a few bucks working in here? I need someone to take baking out of the oven and keep the display racks full."

"I could sure use some spare cash."

"Can we start from ten to two o'clock? It's a bit better than minimum wage, plus free coffee break snacks. Cinnamon buns even!"

"Thanks for thinking of me, Peg. I'll be here before ten tomorrow then."

"I know I can count on you. You're from a good family— you're all good stock. Everyone knows that."

"I didn't expect that," Kate said as Peg left, "but I'm pretty pumped."

Peg's words about family bounced in Polly's head until Jackson spoke. "I'll pick you up at the store tonight. What time do you close on a Friday?"

"'Mrs. Bentley will come in tonight to help Sophia. I can leave any time after six."

"Then I'll be waiting for you. Can I take you to Colonel Butler's for a quiet dinner? Just the two of us."

"It's alright, I'm not offended," Kate joked. "But we're still going shopping today, right?"

As Jackson and Kate left, a new different weight was on his heart, one he hadn't known before.

She's kind and caring and understands me. I had given up on finding love, and she's opened a door that I thought was shut. I'm intertwined with this family now and they need me as much as I need them. I pray she feels the same way about me.

In the few minutes in the car, Jackson refreshed his plan in his mind. First was to coerce Kate's help. He'd come to know her as a kindred spirit who was rooting for Polly's happiness.

Kate was in pins and needles, eager and curious about the day as she waited outside the school's drop off lanes for Jackson's truck.

Whatever is happening, I'm sure it's romantic. What else could it be?

At last, Jackson swallowed hard, knowing what he was going to say to Kate couldn't be taken back. He'd toyed with the idea through the night, repeating the words aloud while staring at the bedroom ceiling. Now it was up to him.

"Kate, I admire how supportive you are to Polly. I'm so sorry about your parents last year, it must have been a hurtful Christmas without them. I've always thought it is important to draw strength and courage from those around you who love you. Until I met Polly, I kept my feelings and personal pain locked inside."

"It was difficult," she said, "but I've worked through it well. Polly is like a mother and ensures we are well provided for and we can talk to her anytime. I've never seen her as happy in the last year as she is now."

Jackson enjoyed the thought. "I was never fortunate enough to have a sister. If I did, I'd want her to be like you. I adore Polly and I want to take care of her for the rest of my life."

Kate's face glowed, twisting in her seat to hear more.

"I want the blessing from you and Tim before I propose. This affects all of you."

"You're so in!" she screamed. "This is way too cool, Jackson!"

"Would you come with me to the jewelry shop? I'm ready today to buy a special Christmas gift."

There were only two fine jewelers in Lac Maurice and they checked out both before returning to Fournier's on Sugarbush. Squinting closely over the glass case, they both laughed as their heads almost bumped.

His voice shook in a whisper. "What kind of ring would she like?"

"She's sentimental, so something symbolic. If I may be presumptuous, I'd suggest four small diamonds that would represent our family."

"I knew I'd picked the right person to guide me. Let's go inside. We'll be patient and find the perfect one."

The clerk brought out one tray after another, and they quickly dismissed most. Finally, they narrowed it to three, then two rings.

"It's that one, for sure."

Jackson pointed to the center of the velvet tray. Under the spotlight was a brilliant two-carat stone raised in a square setting, with four pink diamonds, one at each corner.

"And you'll want to see the matching wedding band," the clerk suggested.

His heart pounded hearing the word wedding. "Yes, definitely."

With his treasure in his pocket, Kate and Jackson headed out for the Patisserie de Soleil. Their steps were light as they jabbered with childish excitement.

The ornate, screened cottage door hinge squeaked as it opened and then sprung closed with a familiar slam.

"I love the sounds and smell of this place," Kate said. She chose a discreet corner table away from the window and local gossip.

"Did you know that my mother used to bring me here for Christmas tea every year?"

Jackson was floored. "I had no idea. Now I'm so glad we're here."

"Their Christmas tea is scrumptious, with these savory petit fours my Mother adored."

"With those tempting descriptions, perhaps you should make the selections for us."

She sat up taller and raised her pinky with a laugh. "Sure, I've become a real tea connoisseur."

Jackson and Kate shared jokes and old memories as they supped, creating a moment she knew she would never forget with this man she'd hoped would enter their forever family.

"Shall I drive you home or will you stay in town?"

"I'll find my own way home, Jackson. Thanks for this once in a lifetime morning."

Kate reached up and planted a kiss on his cheek. "I'll be rooting for you."

An hour later, he was at the rib place waiting for Tim, his hand over the pocket with the little box.

"Hey, Jackson!" Tim called from the door.

"You're early. You must be hungry."

"Ribs are my favs. I've already memorized the menu."

He slid the wooden menu board across to the server. "I'll have a full rack of back ribs with fries and coleslaw."

"The same for me, but a half order," Jackson said.

"What's up that we are having a private lunch?"

"You were joking this morning at the table, teasing that Polly and I should get married. What if I were to propose to your sister . . . would you have any objection?"

Tim became giddy. "I wasn't joking. I'd get a big brother after all and I'd be a fool to object. My sister deserves a good man that will love her and look after her for the rest of her life. If you can do that, you have my vote."

Jackson dug into his pocket. "Kate and I went to the jeweler this morning. I hope you like it too. Kate said the four stones symbolize our family coming together."

"Yeah, that's Kate . . . sentimental. No kidding Jackson, it's beautiful."

Devouring his ribs, Tim talked incessantly about things they could do together in the future as a family, then about his school and ambitions, and family vacations. Jackson listened to every word, feeling an honor bestowed on him from this boy who was still struggling with the loss of his parents.

"Listen, Tim, I'm due at the police station in ten minutes. Can you find your own way home?"

"Sure. Thanks, man!"

Tim slapped Jackson on the back, with the same meaning as Kate's kiss on the cheek.

"And not a word to Polly, as I'll wait until Christmas."

Jackson took a sigh of relief.

"The first step is done."

18

"Well, Lieutenant, it looks like we caught the arsonist red-handed. Has a hearing been set yet?"

"No, he'll stay in the jailhouse over Christmas."

"Ahem…Would it be possible . . . I was wondering . . . you see, Polly Perkins is related to Harris Winslow. She is feeling remorseful and hospitable to her cousin. She asked if I could take him, under my custody, to have Christmas dinner with her family. Everyone deserves a Christmas."

"That's absurd, Jackson. Well at the least highly irregular. We haven't determined yet if he is a flight risk, and he won't get bail until the New Year."

Lieutenant Thorne stretched back in his chair with his hands clasped as he twiddled his thumbs.

"Well, it is Christmas and it does sound callous to leave a bloke in a cell while the rest of the town is fattening up on a turkey feast. I'll see if the Captain will be onboard with your suggestion." His stern face turned warmer, then to a smile.

Jackson had expected obstacles. "I'm prepared to put up a bond. It would only be for two hours at the most."

"I admire your compassion at Christmas. Give me a few minutes to mull it over and I'll have to call Montreal to get a sign-off."

The afternoon with Wayne was relatively uneventful, with only a shoplifter, a mugging of a homeless man and a minor theft from the gas station. Charges weren't laid in the misdemeanors, with the culprits delivered for a hot meal to the Community Kitchen. At the door, Jackson gave his own donation in the box.

At the end of his shift, Jackson was ready to get Polly when Thorne summoned him.

"Jackson, I've come to a decision. On Christmas Day, the Lac Maurice jail is now only hosting two patrons, Harris Winslow and a homeless mugger where the alleged humbug victim refuses to drop the charges.

We'd like to treat our employees as well as we can. To do that, if you would take both patrons for two hours, it would relieve us at the jail and our workers could join their families for dinner. We'll close the jail for that period."

"No problem at all, Sir. We'd be glad to do that."

"You understand, Jackson, that there remains an element of danger. Be prepared and on your guard. Make sure both men are back in their cells by nine."

"Yes, Sir. Thank you, Lieutenant."

Jackson couldn't hide his mischievous smirk when she jumped in the car.

"By your face, it must have been a good day."

"The best. First a lovely tea with Kate, then lunch with Tim, and a talk with Lieutenant Thorne."

Polly clenched her teeth. "I'm afraid to ask."

Jackson explained the outcome. "So it ends up a double order. Ask for one criminal and get two."

She giggled. "You are some negotiator. So who is this mugger we are feeding?"

"A homeless bloke down and out on his luck at Christmas no less. He was probably trying to scoff enough money to drown his misery in liquor."

"Well, I love the idea." She leaned over for a kiss. "Can we stop by the bakery? I'll need an extra-large yule log."

Colonel Butler's was dressed up for the holidays, with white, starry Christmas lights in the trees and a background music of classical orchestral music.

"It's so elegant and romantic, Jackson. Thank you for bringing me. I love it."

The maître d' winked at Jackson. "We have a nice table in the corner by the fireplace. Come this way." The host's smile was enchanting. "I'll bring the champagne right away."

"You ordered wine already for us? You're a lovely man, Jackson," she said.

He reached across the table for her hand. "Pol, I meant what I said last night."

"And I did too. Of course, I'm a little confused about what's going on today with Kate and Tim."

"I've searched my soul and this is what I have to do. You'll find out everything later. Everyone is entitled to a Christmas secret, right?"

Her eyes sparkled as she wistfully imagined the mystery.

"Jackson, is our house overwhelming? You know, adjusting to all of us, with Kate and Tim too?"

"Absolutely not, I'm learning about the Perkins charm."

"I love you for that," she whispered.

"About Christmas Day, is there anything I can do to help?"

"Extra tables, I guess. We'll put them at the end as our list is growing every day. Dad always kept a stack of folding tables and chairs in the garage. Sometimes we loan them to Rev. Dennison for their church dinners.

"Tim invited the single Mom and her newborn from your ride-along last week. And this is the year Hank and Barbara Moffatt come for Christmas dinner as their kids are away at university or married."

Something was on his mind. "What is it?" she said. "What's bothering you?"

"You know the Lieutenant and I came to an agreement, but I don't even know if Winslow is agreeable. Have you considered that he could refuse the invitation?"

"Well, if the Lieutenant has pulled some strings, Harris kind of has to go along with it. I won't take 'no' for an answer."

"You didn't meet his fury when he was arrested at your place. He's an angry chap with a deep-seated hatred for how life has done him wrong. Harris may not be a pleasant dinner companion."

"My parents taught me to look for the good inside people and not to be too quick to judge. Pain creates a variety of behavioral consequences. I'm sure Harris is a soul worth caring for, at least by his own family."

Jackson nodded slowly without a word, imagining where Jarvis might be, and if he ever thought of his brother.

It hurts every day.

As if Polly could read his thoughts, she asked. "Do you carry a picture of your family? I'd like to see Jarvis."

In his wallet, he found a tattered school picture.

"He's tall and was gangly when I last saw him. This was his last year in school, but he didn't stay to graduate. I suppose his predicament is somewhat like Harris's. But we know where Harris is."

"Where do you suppose Jarvis might be?"

"I used to marvel at how mechanical he was . . . he could fix anything, so I wouldn't be surprised if he worked for a garage or repair shop. He could be in Montreal or Quebec City, or maybe hiked a train to the United States. I always look whenever I come to a new town."

"We'll keep searching, Jackson. One day, just you wait, he'll join us at our Christmas table."

"Forever the optimist!" He tightened his hold on her hand.

"Can I keep his picture for a day or two? I like researching at the library and maybe something will come up."

She folded a receipt from her purse around the ragged photo and tucked it inside her pocketbook.

Several townsfolk patrons at Butler's stopped to extend their Christmas wishes to Jackson or Polly as they passed by the table.

"I asked Arnie for a quiet corner table," Jackson joked.

"This is perfectly fine. I enjoy the spirit of our small town and the camaraderie in the community. Being involved helps to fill a void for folks, especially at the holidays."

"I understand that," he said. "Although I'm generally surrounded by people, I can even feel lost and lonely in the midst of it."

"Everyone says time heals all wounds, but I don't think the pain of losing Mom and Dad will ever diminish."

"Nor should you, Polly. You're right to cherish their memories and your senses of a familiar hat or hairdo, or the scent of aftershave or perfume."

"I remember all of those," she whispered.

"Now that you're in my life, you should never feel alone again, Pol. I can never take away your feeling of loss, but I can help build a new sense of belonging . . . to me."

Polly closed her eyes, pondering his words.

"What a wise man you are!"

"I was hoping you'd say you feel the same for me."

"Of course, I do, Jackson. You should know by now that I've fallen in love with you. I couldn't imagine life without you. In our whirlwind romance, I'm guilty of love at first sight."

"I love you too, Pol."

"You need to save some compliments for tomorrow night. I'll be wearing one of my mother's gowns and her accessories. It'll be like she's with me in a way."

As they sipped champagne and shared old stories long into the evening, Jackson suddenly realized the room had emptied out and fallen silent. He rose awkwardly from his chair and went down on one knee.

Polly gasped, stunned that the moment she'd longed for was about to happen. Tears began to sting her eyes and she couldn't understand why she was trembling.

He removed the velvet box from his jacket and stammered to begin.

"Polly . . . Polly Perkins, you are my soulmate and my heart. I love you now and promise to love you more with each day. You've welcomed me into your family with open arms, and both Kate and Tim have given me their blessing that we will be a complete family. Will you marry me?"

Behind the strength of this handsome man, Polly saw the sweet innocence of a schoolboy asking for his first prom date, and tears streamed as she tried to talk.

A soft whisper was all she could manage as she rose to embrace him.

"Of course, Jackson. You're the only man I could ever love."

19

The morning sun drifted through the bedroom window to awaken her. She jolted upright and raised her hand to the sunlight. Without getting out of bed, she called, "Kate! Tim! Come quickly!"

Still in flannel PJs, Kate slid into the room. "Did he ask?"

Polly waved her ring finger, moving the sparkling glint across the ceiling. Tim sauntered in with a sheepish grin.

"Not a bad token!" he joked. "Do I have to call him Dad or what?"

Polly threw her slipper at him in jest.

"Alright crew, she commanded. All hands on deck, this is Christmas Eve. How many people do we have now for dinner?" Polly commanded.

"Two plus me," Kate said.

"And four plus me," Tim added.

"Plus Jackson, Harris, the Moffatts, the mugger and me."

"The Mugger?" Kate spurted in laughter. "And Harris?"

"Harris Winslow is my cousin. From the Saab incident and the police. It turns out he's my kin looking for us. I know Mom and Dad wouldn't have any of our relatives sitting in a jail cell on Christmas Day. Jackson arranged with the Lieutenant to bring him here for dinner and the deal included the mugger."

Kate laughed again. "You mean he's going to look like Red Skelton?"

Polly's voice cracked into laughter at the scenario.

"There's a list on the kitchen table of chores for today. Take your pick. I have to get to town right away and take care of some urgent business and I'll be back before noon."

In blue jeans and a cable sweater, she bounded down to the car. Saturday morning was chilly and clear of traffic lights as she headed to the town's library.

With a computer sign-on, she searched all the garages listed in Prescott, Grenville and Argenteuil Townships and checked any employee lists.

Mrs. Sutcliffe was patient, but as the clock was nearing the noon hour she approached Polly.

"I'm sorry, but for Christmas Eve we're scheduled to close at noon. Perhaps I could give you a quick hand. What is it you're looking for?"

"Thanks, Myrna. It's a mechanic by the name of Jarvis Tripp who once lived in Lac Maurice. I'm at my wit's end."

"There is a directory of all the licensed mechanics in the Eastern Townships. I have it in the back stacks, and it will just take a second."

Myrna ambled away and from beyond the shelves, she returned with a heavy volume.

"If he's a mechanic, either licensed or apprenticing, he's in here." She hummed as she thumbed.

"Tripp, Jarvis . . . why he's not far away at all. Shows him to be at Lac-Brome. I've got the address and phone."

Myrna was puffed with success and gave Polly a pat on the back. "I have a nephew coming from Lac-Brome today for Christmas. If he misses the four o'clock train there's another at ten in the morning. Good luck, Polly. There's a pay phone in the lobby."

With a handful of coins, she placed her call to Goussain's Garage in Lac-Brome. A deep voice answered on the second ring.

"Hello, is this Jarvis Tripp from Lac Maurice?"

The voice hesitated. "Yes, at one time, but I prefer to be called John Doe, depending on what this is about."

Polly went on to explain who she was, how she found him and the reason for her call.

After a long space of silence, Jarvis replied. "Thank you, Polly. You've been very kind, but it's been too long for me and Jackson. I'll think it over."

"Whether you decide to come or not, I'm sending a prepaid train ticket to the depot so you can have Christmas Day with us. Tomorrow morning's train arrives at 11:30 a.m. in Lac Maurice and I'll be on the platform waiting for you. Merry Christmas!"

Too excited to focus on her morning schedule, Polly debated between crying and laughing. Reminding herself that the decision was yet to be made, she didn't want to get Jackson's hopes up. It would be a Christmas Day surprise.

The next hour was filled with errands and parcels before she stopped in at Treasure Box to see Sophia.

"Merry Christmas, Soph. You've got kiddies at home, so let's close up shop. I'll finish up here."

Polly's smile hadn't faded, and she waved her ring finger.

"By gosh, girl, what's that you have?"

"I'm so happy, Sophia. He's the only man in the whole world for me. I never thought I could be this happy. I've been dying to tell you, but everything is so busy. We'll have a good catch-up after Christmas."

"I'm so thrilled for you, Pol. How big is your Christmas dinner now?"

"Somewhere in the neighborhood of seventeen or eighteen. That's still less than when Mom and Dad were here and all the relatives came. I have a couple of surprises up my sleeve. I can't tell you about my devious attempt to bring an unexpected guest as I wouldn't want to jinx it."

"By golly, girl, you do keep me on my toes! Have a Merry Christmas and I hope everything works out. Congrats on the engagement!"

Turning down the CD player, silence echoed through the high ceiling of the Treasure Box.

Polly looked around as if viewing it for the first time. The garland and decorations still held their luster, but in a few days the whizzing of the trains and their whistles would soon be packed up and forgotten.

Scents of pine and bayberry lingered but the quiet and strange emptiness of Christmas Eve was overwhelming.

"Pops, if you can hear me, I want you to know a wonderful man has entered my life. He'll see to it that we are all taken care of in a loving home. You would like him. Don't worry, Pops, he will never take your place . . . I miss you so much at Christmas time."

Coincidentally, a wicker wreath with tiny golden bells and red baubles fell from its place and landed on the floor.

"I love you too, Dad."

Polly went to gather up the remnants, turned on the night lights and locked the front door.

"I have a ball to go to." She giggled with excitement.

Every corner of her house on Maple Drive was filled with the scent of Christmas. Barely inside, Polly stopped to inhale the atmosphere.

"Cinnamon spice and mulled wine! Kate, I'm so glad you remembered. I'd forgotten all about the mulling brew."

"Tim is stuffing the bird," Kate said. "He's using Mom's recipe for apricot sausage stuffing with pecans. Don't tell him, but he did a magnificent job, Polly."

"It would go to his head, but I might say it anyway."

"And the bakery called and Tess said she'd deliver the yule log on her way home as they were closing up."

"I feel this will be one of the best Christmases, Kate."

"Now, Polly, disappear and have a bubble bath and get gussied up. Your fiancé will be here in a few hours."

"My fiancé. Sounds nice."

So much has happened in twenty-four hours, now the ball and the Christmas Day. It's moving so fast. I wish it could be in slow motion.

"You are a vision, Polly," Jackson declared on his first sight of her on the staircase. He carried a chilled corsage and raised his right hand to her with his palm upward as she slowly flowed down to take it.

The jade silk gown hung from her hips like a shimmering fountain, and her Grandmother Perkin's diamond cluster necklace lay gently on her milky, porcelain neck accenting the scooped line of the bodice.

"And you are gracious with your compliments. Thank you, my darling Jackson."

"Life has changed so much. I never knew I could have these feelings," he said.

Huge snowflakes were melting on the limo glass as it glided out the lane onto Maple Street.

"Everyone talks about Mrs. Warner's Snowy Mountain Ball," said Polly. "It's a dream, and a peek into my parents' memories too. Mrs. Warner was so kind and down to earth. Often we misjudge those with money without seeing their real hearts and souls. And I must confess I'd like to see the splendor of our antique candlesticks at the ball. I still have an attachment to them."

"You do find the best in people's souls."

Near Warner's mansion, there was a backup of other chauffeur-driven sedans, as they insisted on third-party transportation to prevent an impairment after a party.

The Warner estate was especially glorious at Christmas, majestic on the top of the hillside, and covered tonight in a light dusting of snow. Cascades of twinkling red, blue, green and yellow lights draped the firs in the courtyard and tall oaks from the main road up the drive to the grand portico entrance. A handful of tuxedoed doormen stood by the pillars ready to spring into service.

Inside the grand foyer, Polly and Jackson were greeted by Mrs. Warner, dressed as a snow queen and dripping with pearls and diamonds.

"Good evening, Mrs. Warner. I'm so pleased to introduce you to my fiancé, Jackson Tripp."

The smile faded from her face and she elbowed her husband and whispered to him, "I believe this would be Meredith's son."

Mr. Warner's dignified persona waivered and his face muscles tightened. A bead of sweat formed on his eyebrows as he stared at Jackson.

Polly's face flushed with embarrassment that something was awry. "We are so sorry if I've caused a distraction from your party, Mr. and Mrs. Warner."

"Oh no, dear. You are more than welcome."

Mrs. Warner stiffened then regained her composure. "Perhaps after the guests have all arrived we could have a nice chat . . . I'll explain later. I do apologize, Polly. And to you too, Jackson. You must both have some champagne and hors-d'oeuvres in the meantime." She waved to a server.

Polly was still stunned and Jackson put his arm around her waist. "Come to the ballroom, my darling."

"What's that all about, Jackson? I don't understand."

"I didn't think it was relevant. My mother used the name of Meredith Carter when she worked at the mansion. It was many years ago and I'm surprised the Warners would make any connection to me."

The glamour of the night had been instantly overshadowed for Polly. She was still simmering from the earlier news of the Tripp family's past and was now floored by the revelation that Meredith Carver was the beloved maid of Mrs. Warner.

At a midpoint of the evening, the Warners together approached the couple.

"Please call us Alexander and Claire," she said. "Your parents knew us that way, Polly."

Alexander's face still showed anguish, and he listened as his wife spoke.

"My dear, I owe you an apology. You're a vision of your mother tonight and it does my heart good to have you here in her place."

She turned to her husband. "Alexander, perhaps you should explain further."

Alexander Warner was a distinguished man of eighty years, with excellent posture and manners reflecting a life of grandeur and dignity. He swallowed hard before he began.

"I concur with my wife, Polly. You look ravishing. But it's to you, Jackson, that I owe my explanation and heartfelt regret. This is difficult to come face-to-face with in this unexpected moment, and I beg your patience to listen to a story that should have been told long ago."

Jackson squeezed Polly's hand. "Please, Sir, at your leisure if you have something you wish to tell me."

The Warner's demeanors softened. "You have an ancestor Wilhelmina Hanson that I'm sure you've heard of."

"My grandmother . . . yes."

"Wilhelmina was beautiful and had the same warm brown eyes as you have, with a hint of sparkling emeralds. I admit I was enthralled as a young man . . . of course long before your time, Son."

Mrs. Warner leaned forward squeezing her husband's arm with encouragement.

"We knew it when we saw your eyes!"

"Jackson, I was betrothed to Wilhelmina before the War but then I was sent overseas. As a soldier, I wouldn't let her promise to wait for me. When I returned after the War, I found that she had married another and they had a child, a beautiful, little girl, also with brown eyes. That was Meredith.

I had my suspicions I was the father, but Wilhelmina was adamant that Meredith was her new husband's child."

Warner's eyes darted back and forth between Jackson and Claire.

"I fell in love with my dear Claire and we went on with our life in Lac Maurice. I always wondered about Meredith, then one day she applied to work here. I was so blessed to see her coming up the lane every morning. I soon heard that she was in an abusive marriage and had two young boys. I explained my suspicions with Claire and she went to see Wilhelmina one day to find the truth."

Polly sensed the mounting emotion and interjected, "May I presume that Meredith was definitely your daughter?"

Mr. Warner nodded. "We spoke with Meredith one day about her parentage and she was in denial and resigned her position here. It was a tragedy for all of us. It had been a gift to have her in our household, to see her every day."

Claire smiled lovingly. "You see, Jackson, you are our grandson!"

Jackson's mind went blank and his heart pounded, but he found the strength to stammer a reaction.

"I never knew!"

Polly knew he needed help. "That is wonderful, Mr. and Mrs. Warner. Everyone should be embraced by their own kin." She was not only thinking of Jackson's brother but of her cousin.

"We're sorry if we ruined your party in any way," Jackson said. "Mr. and Mrs. Warner, I need to have some time to myself to sort this out."

Polly could see that these three hearts were suffering from longing and fear, and her impetuousness to heal souls took over.

"Thank you for the courage to tell Jackson such precious news. Perhaps it's best to have time to get acquainted with our thoughts."

"Of course," said Mrs. Warner.

"But if I can be so forward, we're having a dinner party tomorrow. Some folks there have broken hearts that need mending. I'll leave the decision to Jackson, but if he should ask you to come tomorrow, would you be agreeable? It's just family and special friends."

Mrs. Warner took Polly in her arms with tears streaming. "Thank you, dearest."

Alexander remained composed but couldn't hide his pain and his love for his grandson.

"We'll wait to hear from you, Jackson. I'm glad we finally got to meet. You've always been in my heart and now we open our home and family to you. I should have done it before."

Jackson asked the valet to summons a limousine. Polly had never seen him so withdrawn and knew his guard was up. On the way, he peered out at the darkness in silence.

Overwrought, he sagged into Seymour's armchair, and Polly brought him a spice tea.

On a Christmas radio station. Grandpa Jones was reciting an old German folktale, *The Christmas Guest*. He turned his head to listen to the last stanza.

Lift up your head, for I kept my word
Three times my shadow crossed your floor
Three times I came to your lonely door
For I was the beggar with bruised, cold feet
And I was the woman you gave somthin' to eat

And I was the child on the homeless street.
Three times I knocked and three times I came in
And each time I found the warmth of a friend.
Of all the gifts, love is the best."

"I love you with my full heart, Polly, but I don't know how to deal with this."

She eased onto his lap and kissed him. "You were right when you said you needed time to think."

"Does time really heal?"

"You're a wise and loving man. You've taken in three people from this house to be your family and we all love you. Life is brief and we must grasp joy in whatever form it comes. The house will be bustling in the morning and I accept whatever will be your decision."

"Thank you, dear Polly."

"Goodnight, my love!"

20

Polly set her alarm for six to sneak downstairs and hang the stockings by the fireplace then fill them with small gifts she had collected in recent weeks.

In Tim's stocking, she put her grandfather's heirloom pocket watch inside a jeweler's box. For Kate, she deposited a new leather diary with a key lock, and for Jackson, she placed the newly polished locket from the treasure box, signifying his grandparents.

Each stocking was filled to the top and overflowing with nuts, fruit, trinkets, miniature toys, puzzles and the hand-knitted mittens Polly bought in town.

She crept back up the stairs and crawled back into bed, into a deep, satisfying sleep until the smell of bacon and the sound of laughter awoke her from her dreams.

This would be the first Christmas morning her father hadn't burst through her bedroom door singing *I Heard the*

Bells on Christmas Day to drag her out of bed as he rang the dinner bell from the kitchen.

"Let's see if Santa came, Pumpkin!" his voice boomed even when she was an adult.

Grabbing her robe, she bounded down the stairs.

"Good morning, sleepy head!" Jackson stood over a frying pan wearing Mrs. Perkin's apron. "We are starting a new tradition for Christmas morning. The men in the house make breakfast."

Tim appeared from the pantry with muffins and a platter of fruit. "Yeah, Polly, whatever he says rules."

She wrapped her arms around the back of Jackson.

After everything Jackson was through yesterday, how do I tell him we are picking up a surprise passenger at the train station at 11:30? Maybe yes and maybe no.

When Kate arrived, Jackson surprised everyone.

"Good morning, future sister-in-law. Do you mind setting the dinner table for two more guests?"

"Awesome! Who's coming?"

"My Grandpa is bringing Mrs. Warner."

"Wow, the chauffeur Mr. Withers is your Grandpa?"

Jackson and Polly burst in laughter, knowing everything was alright. A quick story of Warners' Ball was passed on to Tim and Kate, who were both stunned and delighted that the family had grown overnight.

"Kate, maybe make the settings for three more, not two."

"You guys are full of surprises. Who's the third?"

"Yes, Polly, who's the third?" Jackson said.

"If I told you, it wouldn't be a surprise. Come with me to the train station. We have a pickup at 11:30."

"Are we all going?" Kate asked.

"No, you and Tim need to keeping peeling vegetables, the surprise is just for Jackson right now."

During the whirr of morning activity, Polly noticed that Jackson was becoming almost giddy in his curiosity about the pickup.

"Come on, Pol, it's eleven already and we should get going. The War is over and the troops are coming home!"

What an odd thing to say . . . he couldn't know.

With a light snowfall, the roads were clear, with little traffic for Christmas morning. Jackson pulled into the train station at 11:20. Checking his watch, he hurried Polly up to the promenade.

"You know my shift starts at one?"

"Yes, I know. This shouldn't take too long."

"Here comes a train. Who should we be looking for?" Jackson leaned forward peering down the bend as a locomotive eased into the station.

A flood of passengers disembarked with parcels and bags, with laughter and hugs of families and friends. The crowd dispersed and Jackson stood gaping at a young man wearing a leather bomber jacket and a satchel standing at the end of the platform in trepidation.

"Jarvis? Is it really you?" Jackson bounded toward his brother.

"By gosh, Jackson, you've gotten old," Jarvis quipped. Polly stayed back, enjoying the sight of a marvelous reunion until it struck Jackson about the logistics.

"Pol, how did you do it? Jarvis, this is my fiancé, Polly Perkins."

"She's quite a gal, Jackson. I'm as stubborn as they come and she managed to convince me to be on this train."

Jarvis extended his hand and she surprised him with a sudden embrace. "Merry Christmas!"

When Kate and Tim heard the car pull into the drive, they raced to the front door brimming with curiosity. There was no need for introductions, the family similarity was so strong.

In the comfort of the Perkins house, Jarvis began to come to life. "I've been a loner so long," he said to Jackson. "Be patient with me?"

"Come on a ride-along on this afternoon's shift. There's a lot to catch up on and the start of a new chapter."

He hesitated and looked to Polly. "I love you for this. The best is yet to come, Pol—the day you become my wife and we begin our lives together."

In the depth of his eyes at that moment, she caught a glimpse not only of his soul but of Jeremiah, Wilhelmina, Alexander, and Meredith.

There's passion in that group!

Soon after six p.m., guests began arriving, bearing mince tarts and poinsettias, wrapped gifts and glazed hams.

Kate's friend Monica and her grandmother were first there, eager and expounding gratitude to be included. Next were neighbors Hank and Barbara Moffatt, who come on alternate years when their grown children spend holidays with the in-laws.

Hugs were exchanged between the strangers as if they were all old friends.

Polly kept watch on the window for Warner's car and second-guessed that Withers should have been included.

Surprisingly, it was Mr. Warner himself who arrived in a classic Bentley from the fifties. It purred slowly into the lane.

"Wow! Look at that, Polly. Who is it?" Tim slipped to the veranda for a better look, then a gentlemanly instinct jumped into play and he rushed to help the two elderly people struggle out of the car.

"Good evening, young man. Would you be so kind as to assist Mrs. Warner?"

Alexander Warner was panting from pulling himself out of the soft, luxurious seats and pushing on the heavy door. As Tim opened Mrs. Warner's side, Alexander fumbled through his billfold sensing a tip was in order.

"No, no, Sir. You're our guest."

Mrs. Warner reached out a sleek black glove and stepped out in a lengthy fur-trimmed black coat and a black feathered fascinator over her silver bouffant.

"Are you one of the Hansons?" she asked.

"Oh, no. I'm a Perkins. Timothy Perkins."

"Thank goodness. We're the Warners. We're Jackson's grandparents!"

Tim smiled kindly at the sudden attachment.

"We couldn't be happier to have you both join us today. Merry Christmas, Mrs. Warner."

Tim gently guided her toward the veranda where Polly was helping Mr. Warner as he navigated the stairs with the support of a walking stick.

Within earshot, Tim whispered, "Polly, these are the Warners. Aren't they wonderful?"

Instantly they became the center of attention with a charming display of their warmth, wit, and humor from a lifetime of social events.

Jackson, I wish you were here to see this . . . the old and young mixing so well. There's so much joy in the house already.

As she checked the clock and the guest list, her nerves tensed, realizing that not only Jackson and Jarvis would be here soon for dinner . . . but Harris too, and the mugger.

She picked up the hall phone after the first ring, hoping it would be Jackson.

"Polly. It's me. We're leaving the station. However the chaplain stopped by to visit the prisoners, and I sort of had to invite him too."

He clenched her teeth in a nervous laugh. "Of course, the chaplain should come. It might be a suitable balance between the Warners and the mugger."

"Polly you are doing a wonderful, selfless thing."

Harris Winslow hung his head in shame on the front steps. Polly stepped outside at the sound of the car to avoid an awkward moment for Harris inside.

"Hello, Polly . . ." He was clenching his hat and wrung it tight.

"I'm thankful we could arrange for you to be with us for Christmas Dinner. It's time to start all over with our getting acquainted."

She was sensitive to his state of mind, that he would be carrying humiliation at facing the family. "My siblings share this sentiment too. You are very welcome, Harris."

His grey eyes softened and a smile replaced the scorn and hatred from before.

"I haven't had a family dinner since a teenager when I was kicked out of the Winslow house."

"Come in, Harris. I want you to meet the rest of our extended family and friends."

"First, Polly, I apologize. I'm ashamed for what I've put you and your family through. I'm sorry about Aunt Maddie and Uncle Seymour. I hadn't heard of their passing until recently."

The chaplain quickly attuned himself to the diverse backgrounds of the guests and provided a sympathetic ear for Harris. He stayed close to the mugger with an eye always on him, one of the Lieutenant's conditions.

Clearing his throat and tinkling a spoon on a water goblet, the chaplain thanked Polly and her family for opening their doors to this mosaic of guests then prayed their thanksgiving for the bountiful feast.

Chatter and laughter consumed the guests as great bowls and cauldrons of vegetables were passed in all directions.

From the table's end, Jackson wielded the carving knife, doling generously portions from the platters of turkey and ham.

"Grandpa, would you like a leg or white meat?"

Alexander Warner was befuddled until Claire cupped his ear and whispered, "You're Grandpa!"

"Yes, indeed Jackson, I would enjoy the leg." He passed his plate. "If I may say, this is marvelous. We usually have leftover cold cuts and salads that the cook leaves for us at Christmas." He chuckled at the irony of his misfortune. "It's been years since we sat down at an old-fashioned Christmas dinner."

Kate asked, "When Jackson and Polly get married, I guess you'll kind of be our grandpa too?"

The Warners laughed thoroughly at the family banter and teasing, and Alexander unbuttoned his vest to loosen his tie.

Tim piped up, "Well, Mr. Warner, I'm so glad that you came. You see Jackson told us that his grandfather was coming with Mrs. Warner and I thought it was Withers!"

Claire loosened up with a roar that started contagious fits and rolls of laughter that circled the table, with Mr. Warner almost choking from his turkey and collapsing from his chair.

The commotion finally died down to intermittent snickers and chortles, and eventually, everyone took long sighs and resumed passing the platters.

Jarvis, at last relaxed, began piecing together the story of his reunion. "Well, Mr. and Mrs. Warner, if Jackson is your grandson, then so am I, right?"

Wide-eyed, Alexander put down his fork-full of ham, and together the Warners looked to Jackson in confusion.

"Indeed you are," Jackson said.

"Grandpa and Grandma Warner, this is Jarvis, my brother. Two is better than one."

The table hushed as Alexander Warner looked at the young man with immediate acceptance.

"Dear Jarvis, it is a delight to know you. I've explained the story several times but the basic facts are that I am your mother's biological father . . . my dear Meredith."

It was another bombshell for Jarvis, a Christmas miracle, after so many years of abandonment to have this strange family welcome him as their own.

"It is indeed a grand day for all of us," Mr. Warner declared.

"There's more," Jackson said. He stood from his chair and dug into his pocket. He glanced at Polly, who already knew his thoughts.

"Grandpa Warner, I received a precious gift in my stocking this year that I feel should belong to you. The engravings on the back are W.H. and A.W., and I believe that would be you and Wilhelmina."

The old man's hands trembled as he reached out.

"My goodness, this is the locket I gave to Wilhelmina before I left for enlistment overseas."

It was clear that Alexander had gone back to a special place in his mind and heart to his first love.

"Dear Alexander, you are a lucky man to have two true loves, but my love is forever," Mrs. Warner whispered, slipping her hand into his.

Kate turned up *I'll be Home for Christmas* on the stereo, and Hank Moffatt's voice boomed over the din and crescendo of chatter and laughter. "Although we're not kin, I hope we're invited again next year."

He stood and lined up the Warners, Tripps, and Perkins for a portrait by the tree. Knowing they'd return to their jail cells any minute, Harris Winslow and the mugger both squeezed into the photo, still in crepe hats from the table crackers.

Harris took a bold and humbling step up beside Polly and Tim. "Thank you, Perkins family, for helping those less fortunate. I'll never be the same. It's my best Christmas!"

"Hear, hear," said Polly with her hand in Jackson's. "It's ours too. Merry Christmas, everyone!"

With newfound acceptance, Hank spontaneously took center stage in front of the portrait contingent and appointed himself choir director.

"Come on, sing it, everyone . . . On the first day of Christmas, my true love gave to me."

Polly watched Jackson's face as it lit up on each chorus, getting louder and more rambunctious with each verse. Each time, his voice could be heard high above the others, clear as a bell, as he sang passionately of the 'two turtle doves'.

The End

About the Author

Shirley Burton is a Canadian author in fiction genres, including suspense thrillers in the Thomas York Series, old-fashioned whodunit capers in Inspector Furnace Mysteries, and nostalgic, family-oriented Christmas stories. Journey on her historical fiction from France in the 1500s, and let your imagination take you on the inspiring fantasy adventure *Boy from Saint-Malo*.

Shirley's residence is in Niagara-on-the Lake, Ontario, and Calgary, Alberta.

"I've been privileged to explore the locations of my books, walking the characters' neighborhoods and streets. Research has taken me to Istanbul, France, Italy, Greece, London, Amsterdam, Brazil, California, New York, and Quebec.

"Join me in my 600-page historical fiction, *Homage: Chronicles of a Habitant*, that portrays ten generations of a typical family migrating from France to the New World, paralleling real-world events over 500 years.

"There comes a time in life to take the leap into writing. It's that time for me."

Shirley Burton

shirleyburtonbooks.com

CLOCKMAKER'S CHRISTMAS

A nostalgic Christmas story for all ages. A mother of two small children travels from Manhattan to Heidelberg to resolve an estate. In the magical setting of the Castle and the Christmas markets, she is tempted into a whirlwind romance. With matchmaking charm, a clockmaker bestows unique gifts on the couple. A feel-good, old-fashioned Christmas.

THE WISH STORE

An inspiring Christmas story in charming Chimney Ridge, Vermont. Rudy Hancock's Emporium is the town's focal point, with toys and imagination. It becomes the town's wish store at Christmas, turning wishes into miracles and deeds. With a lad helping as an elf, Rudy and the townsfolk fulfill the wishes of a veteran, a musician, a widow, a young girl, and a wanderer, celebrating at the Fezziwig Ball.

A WENCESLAS CHRISTMAS

A Christmas story of love and charity in the French Alps near Chamonix at a centuries-old luxury hotel. Chef Marceau's niece catches the eye of the sous-chef, sparking a romance. Following an avalanche and a family isolated in the mountains, a spirit of charity grows at the hotel, inspired by tales of the Good King Wenceslas. Together, the employees and guests carry the Wenceslas spirit into the village.

CHRISTMAS TREASURE BOX

Polly Perkins operates the family antique shop. In the days before Christmas, she finds her grandmother's diaries, revealing a lost love she had held from others in her life. Polly meets a man who whisks her into a romance. A distant relative claims on the family's resources, and Polly pursues a resolution toward a memorable Christmas Day.

SECRET CACHE

Book Four of THE THOMAS YORK SERIES. A young man vacationing in Brazil is kidnapped and conned into participating in a bank robbery. Years later, one of the captured thieves set on revenge seeks the cash booty taken, leading him to a California vineyard with a connection. Thomas and Rachel race from Paris to Napa Valley to assist in a murder investigation of her Uncle Zach.

THE PARIS NETWORK

Book Five of THE THOMAS YORK SERIES. The young protagonists, Thomas and Rachel, are back in Paris. After the Bataclan terrorist attack, an encounter at the Basilica in Montmartre sets them on the track of a terrorist plot to collapse the catacomb system in Paris with a drone scheme. A former Interpol agent comes to their aid when Rachel's life is at risk. A contemporary story of terror and suspense.

THE MASQUERADE

Book Six of THE THOMAS YORK SERIES, in Paris. Thomas and Rachel receive an invitation to the French palace's annual costumed ball to diffuse a ransom heist to secure Napoleon artifacts tied to museum criminals. But all is not as it seems as they return to the events and culprits of an unsolved Paris scaffold heist from seven years before.

RED JACKAL

A thriller in Istanbul and on a Mediterranean cruise. Finn receives a letter from an Afghanistan war comrade, enticing him to retrieve an Ottoman artifact stolen from a Sultan's tomb. He infiltrates a smuggling ring to flush out the criminals. Double agents keep him on the run with the attractive Nicole Colbert, and he'd do anything to save her.

EPITAPH OF AN IMPOSTER

A suspense mystery with an imposter, a blackmailer, and unscrupulous members of the House of Lords. The astute collector of rare books in London comes upon an incriminating set of post-war journals of stuffy Lord Tannahill, with secrets of past crimes and of an imposter who crept into the Tannahill family. The bookseller conspires with an employee to expose a blackmail plot, as the drama intertwines past generations linked to an old English manor.

SENTINEL IN THE MOORS

A warm, comical vengeance in a charming setting. A museum archivist, Gabe Farrow, takes a sabbatical at a seaside village, Staithes, in England's North Yorkshire Moors. He discovers a plot to steal a hoard of Viking treasures in the moors. As he befriends the colorful townsfolk, his landlady and a young lad assist him in exposing the plot, testing the village's loyalty.

MYSTERY AT GREY STOKES

An Inspector Furnace Mystery, an old-fashioned whodunit. In an English country manor during Christmas festivities, guests arrive for a splendid feast. The cast includes the butler, housekeeper, the Berwick family members, and social guests. Inspector Furnace and Detective Prentice are called to the manor to untangle the deception and solve the case.

SWINDLE: MYSTERY AT SEA

An Inspector Furnace Mystery whodunit. The Inspector and his bride set out on a sailing on the Queen Elizabeth to New York. A body is found in the cargo, and as Inspector Furnace takes charge, a host of passengers and celebrities become suspects and amateur detectives at the nightly Captain's Table dinner to analyze clues and reveal the culprit.

www.ingramcontent.com/pod-product-compliance
Lightning Source LLC
Chambersburg PA
CBHW050530190726

48284CB00003B/1005